Mayhem

A Deveroux Investigation

Andrew Rowberry

Mayhem

ISBN: 979-8-218-72848-9

CONTENTS

CHAPTER 1

The smell of burnt coffee and fried onions clung to the air like the past to a guilty man. I sat at my usual booth in the back corner of Manny's, a rusted-out diner tucked away at a forgotten intersection. The place had a ghostly hum to it. The kind of hum you don't notice until you realize how quiet the world's become. A neon sign buzzed faintly in the front window, bleeding red light across the linoleum floor in a heartbeat rhythm. I'd been nursing the same cup of coffee for an hour, chewing over the newspaper in front of me like it held any answers.

Most folks get their news piped straight into their skulls by the digital gods of phones, tablets and talking heads on TVs. Not me. I like the sound of pages turning and the texture of cheap ink. I'm old-fashioned that way. Maybe nostalgic. Maybe just stubborn. There was nothing in it but bad news printed cheap. I read it anyway. Habit. Like the way old soldiers shine shoes that won't march anymore.

My plate was cleared, the eggs a distant memory, and the waitress kept refilling my mug like it mattered. It didn't. But it gave me something to hold. Something to keep me from fidgeting. Gary had said she needed help. Said she was in trouble. They always are.

Gary Donovan. A lawyer with more dust than clients and an office wedged between a bail bondsman and a payday loan shop in a part of downtown that had given up hope somewhere around 1987. The carpet in his office reeked of mildew, the walls sweated nicotine, and the receptionist was usually a broken fan whirring from a cracked plastic desk.

We'd met behind O'Malley's Bar the night he almost got his teeth kicked in by a couple of tweakers. I was tailing someone for a cheating-spouse gig and saw two shadows working him over. Turned out the spouse wasn't cheating, he was mugging drunks. I broke one guy's nose, flipped the spouse into a dumpster, and dragged Gary out of the alley. Since then, he's sent me clients out of what he calls loyalty but smells more like penance.

I didn't want to call him my friend, but I wasn't sure what other title to give him. Sometimes I'd use his office to hold things. Sometimes I'd sleep on the couch. When Gary calls, though, it ain't for company. It's because something's broken and bleeding.

That's why I was planted in a booth at Manny's when she walked in.

The bell over the door rang, and the diner's low murmur dropped to a hush. The air shifted. Like fate just decided to wear perfume.

She didn't walk in—she arrived. Every guy in the place turned. Not one of us blamed the others. She wore a tailored black trench coat that cinched at the waist, framing an hourglass silhouette that looked carved from secrets. Beneath it, the hem of a burgundy dress kissed the top of her knees. It was classy, form-fitting, and dangerous in all the right ways. Her heels weren't the kind you wore for comfort, and her walk wasn't the kind that needed excuses. It was measured. Deliberate. Like she knew exactly how many eyes she had and how to keep them.

Her auburn hair spilled around her shoulders in just-managed waves, as if it had been tousled deliberately to look accidental. Her makeup was minimal but sharp with highlighted cheekbones, bold lips. But it was her eyes that pulled you under. Emerald and alive. Eyes that had seen more than she let on.

She approached like a lioness checking for weakness. I didn't stand. I've stood for dames before. It got me scars and unpaid bills.

"You're Deveroux?" she asked. Her voice was velvet-smooth and threaded with just a hint of hesitation.

"That's right," I said, motioning to the seat.

She sat across from me, and for a second, we just studied each other. Like we were both wondering who would flinch first.

"I'm Mary," she said finally. "Mr. Deveroux, I was told you might be able to help. Gary said you take cases that the police dismiss."

"Gary told me you'd be coming."

"I need your help," she said. Her voice tried to sound composed, but the tremble beneath it betrayed her.

"That's what he said."

She leaned forward, and a small silver pendant swayed into view. It was a dove clutching an olive branch in its mouth, delicate and impossibly bright against the darkness of her dress and the tan of her skin. I stared longer than I meant to, hypnotized by its gleam and what it

3

stood for. Peace. Hope. Things that didn't last in my world. She noticed.

"See anything you like?"

I cleared my throat. "Interesting necklace."

"It was mine since I was a child. My father gave it to me when I was eight. Said it symbolized the power of peace even when the world felt like it was breaking. I still wear it. Helps me remember who I used to be."

"Hope gets you killed in this city."

"Or saves you. Depending on who you trust."

"That a warning?"

"A suggestion."

"I understand this is about your roommate?"

"Yes. Stephanie and I had shared a place for over a year. She was bright, generous. Naïve in a way I admired and feared. She believed people were mostly good, just misled. When she met Metal, she saw someone worth saving."

"Who's Metal?"

"He is, was, her boyfriend," she clarified.

"Sounds like you didn't like her choice in men."

Mary's lips twitched. "I saw a predator. He had charm, yes. Money and a nice car, and plenty of charisma. But there was something in his eyes, something hollow. Stephanie said I was being unfair. That I didn't know him. But I knew enough."

"So she came to you?"

"Not exactly. She started avoiding me and didn't come home often. Then one afternoon, she came home shaken. She said she'd seen him beat someone over some kind of drug deal. She said there was nothing she could do because she was in too deep. She didn't want to run, but she

4

didn't want to stay. We argued. The next morning..."

She swallowed hard.

"She was found dead. Car crash. Single vehicle. The police suggested she lost control. But I know better. Her brakes were new and she was sober. And she didn't drive that stretch of road unless she was heading to see him."

"You think someone tampered with her car?"

"I think someone made sure she couldn't talk. And I think the police didn't ask the right questions. Or didn't want to."

"Is the investigation complete?" I asked.

"No. It's still ongoing but I don't think they're taking it as seriously as they should be. I'm afraid they're going to overlook some important information. That's why I need help."

"Why Gary?"

"I met him a while ago and heard he takes cases that other attorney's won't. If the police are being negligent, I want to make sure there are legal ramifications. I told him I went to the police first and laid it all out. They smiled. Nodded. Took a statement. Then filed it in the drawer where inconvenient truths go to die. Gary said you don't scare easy. That you don't look away."

"I don't."

She met my eyes fully then. The tremble was gone. What remained was the steel.

"I want the truth, Mr. Deveroux. I want to know what really happened to her. And I want Metal to pay, if it's what he deserves."

I studied her. Really studied her. The fear was real. So was the grief. But behind it all, there was something else. A quiet fire. She wasn't just looking for peace. She was looking for justice or maybe vengeance.

"I'll take the case."

"Just like that?"

"I've heard enough to know you're not lying. And I don't like people getting pushed around by guys like this Metal."

She smiled, soft and exhausted. "Thank you."

"And call me Steve."

"Alright, Steve."

She left with a warning.

"He's dangerous. He enjoys it."

"So do I, sometimes."

When the door shut behind her, I paid the check, tipped heavy, and stepped into the kind of gray that only a rotting city can offer.

The name was Metal. That's where I'd start.

The city hadn't changed. Trash clung to the gutters like forgotten confessions. Sirens screamed in the distance. Somewhere, someone was bleeding. Somewhere else, someone was lighting a cigarette with stolen matches. This place was alive in the same way tumors are alive. Feeding, spreading, killing.

I drove past the courthouse, past the old church that hadn't held a service in years, past Gary's office where the blinds were always closed. I drove until I couldn't hear Mary's voice in my head anymore.

But it always came back.

Hope for better things.

Sure. And maybe this time, the monsters would stay in the stories.

CHAPTER 2

If you're trying to find a guy like Metal, the worst place to look is where it makes sense. Which is exactly why I went there first.

The address Mary gave me led to a part of the city that looked like it lost a war no one talked about. The pavement was cracked, the windows were boarded, and the air smelled like piss, oil, and lost dreams. If misery had a ZIP code, this would be it.

I parked a block away because I didn't want anyone to see me coming or think there was anything valuable in the car. Around here, they'd strip a vehicle faster than a buzzard on a carcass. I walked the rest of the way, keeping my hands in my coat and my eyes everywhere else.

People swayed down the sidewalk like zombies who'd traded brains for heroin. Hollow eyes, sagging skin, and expressions that said yesterday had been bad and today wasn't trying to do much better. A pair of eyes blinked at me from the shadows of an alley. Hungry. But not stupid.

Daylight still had some power.

I passed a guy in a long coat selling knockoff Rolexes from a velvet tray hanging around his neck. "Got the time, boss?" he said with a grin full of gold caps. "Only ten bucks for the watch to tell it to ya."

I waved him off.

Another block, and a trio of dealers sat on overturned milk crates outside a liquor store. One of them held out a clear bag full of blue tablets. "Candy? Wake ya up, make ya dance?"

"No dancing today."

"Then what you doing around here, old man?" the second sneered.

"Looking for someone worse than you."

That earned a chuckle and a few muttered curses. They didn't get up. Didn't need to. They'd already written me off as a guy not worth the bullet.

A teenage gangbanger watched me cross the street, his crew flanking him like hyenas. He flexed his jaw and made a fake pistol with his fingers, aiming it at me.

"Bang," he whispered. I kept walking.

The building was one of those tenement relics from a better time—back when people still believed concrete could outlive bullets. It loomed like a tired boxer leaning against the ropes, barely standing but not down yet. Metal's last known residence. Tall. Gray. Forgotten.

Near the steps, a pack of miscreants lounged with open contempt. Five of them, sharing a blunt and watching the street like they owned it. Hoodies up, eyes cold, tattoos crawling up their necks.

One with a chipped tooth pointed at me and said, "Look at this guy. Walkin' like he got a badge under that coat."

Another snorted. "Nah. Too clean. Bet he gets lost lookin' for Whole Foods."

A third leaned closer to the door, whispering to the others. "Watch this. Old boy's about to get bounced."

Just as I reached the bottom step, the door to the building exploded open. A guy, maybe early twenties, sandy hair matted with sweat, stumbled out like he'd just been ejected from hell. Frat boy type. Clean jacket, shiny sneakers, breathless. He hit the sidewalk hard, scrambled up like a deer in headlights, and tore off into the street.

The miscreants laughed and jeered. "Told you! They tossing punks again!"

The front door was guarded by a man who looked like he'd been assembled from leftover myth. His chest jutted out like a boulder, his arms could crush a watermelon, and his gut had long since declared independence from the rest of his body. His shoes didn't match. Neither did his eyes or his expression.

"You lost, polo?" he grunted as I stepped up.

I glanced at my button-up shirt. It was pressed and definitely didn't scream money. Either way, it definitely made me stick out. I played it meek. "Actually it's a button-up." His gaze was cold and unchanging. "That's cool. It can be a polo."

"What do you want?" he snarled.

"Heard there might be a place available. Thought I'd take a tour."

"There isn't."

"Then I'll just browse. Maybe something will pop up." I stepped forward. He mirrored me and I stopped.

"There's nothing for you here. Turn around while you're still able to."

"I'm not here to cause trouble."

He grabbed my collar and lifted me like I weighed nothing. I felt the shirt strain, and suddenly I was eye-level with the giant.

"Trouble already found you, little man."

"Little? Six feet isn't tiny. You need to recalibrate."

His fist slammed into my stomach as he let me fall to the ground. My fist tightened and I grit my teeth. I was ready to go on the attack but if Metal, or anyone else was watching, I may lose my chance of getting any more information I needed. I slouched over, gasping for air as he stepped towards me again. I lifted one hand to stop him from taking another strike.

"I was told this is where Metal stays. I just need to talk to him."

He stopped and loomed over me like an animal toying with its meal. "Why should I care?"

"He... he's my cousin. Look, I don't want any trouble, alright? I'm just the guy who gets stuck with the errands nobody wants. He's got something coming to him. Family business."

"That right?" he asked as his curiosity was peaked. "What kind of business?"

"Private kind. I just wanna drop something off, say my piece, and go. You know how families are. Always drama."

He studied me for a long moment, then snatched me by the collar and hoisted me like a cat with a misbehaving kitten. My feet left the pavement.

"So why you looking so nervous if you're family?"

I did my best to stammer. "Hey, hey, look, man. I get it. A big guy like you doesn't want strangers poking around. I respect that. I just don't want to screw this up. Just trying to do what I was told."

That earned a pause. Then a grunt. Then he lowered me.

"First room on the right," he said stepping aside opening the door as if he didn't just threaten to end my life.

I walked into the building and heard the door slam behind me. I glanced back and saw he was talking into a phone. Watching me. Whatever he had planned for me was now in motion. The hall smelled like someone'd mopped the place with urine and bourbon. Graffiti screamed from every wall while music thumped from somewhere above. I kept moving.

The door was unmarked except for a bent number nailed in at an angle. I knocked. It creaked open to reveal a hunched old woman with clouded eyes and no expression.

"Metal's mom?" I asked.

She said nothing, just gave a slow blink. Then, with effort, she stepped aside and shuffled out past me into the hallway, like she'd seen this play before and wanted no part of the next act.

As I turned back to the doorframe, I heard it: "Turn around. Slow."

The voice was dry and shaky. I turned and found myself staring down the barrel of a revolver that looked like it should be mounted on a wall. The guy holding it was a scarecrow in human skin. Hollow face, trembling arm, eyes that hadn't seen peace in years.

"Get inside," he said.

I tried to keep the act going. Shuffled a bit. Hands up, voice a little panicked. "Look, man, I don't want any trouble. I think I got the wrong place, alright? I'll just back away now..."

A heavy bump behind me. I turned and looked at the doorman again.

"You gotta teach me that ninja routine. Seriously."

He didn't laugh. He just threw me forward into the apartment like yesterday's trash.

"Let's talk about that business," the big man purred as he and the scarecrow entered the room, closing and locking the door behind them.

The place was a dump. Rotting furniture, empty bottles, enough drug residue to start a pharmacy. Unfortunately, the type of crowd I was all-too familiar with.

I sighed and pulled out all six bucks in my pocket. "Big inheritance. Try not to spend it all in one place."

They weren't amused.

"He owes us," the scarecrow said.

"I'm sure you're not the only one, either. Good luck collecting. I'll pass the message when I meet him."

"You said you were his cousin," the door man sneered. Bile and anger rose in his voice as he inched towards me.

"Yes, you're right. I did say that." They both stared. I could see the gears grinding in their chemically compromised skulls. "And that was a lie. See, now we're bonding."

"She's gonna be pissed," the scarecrow said.

"She's got enough on her plate," replied the doorman.

"She who?" I asked. It seemed as though more than one person had an issue with Metal which meant my time table to find him had just sped up.

They ignored me.

"What do we do?" Scarecrow asked, hand trembling again.

I raised my hands slowly. I didn't want him twitching too hard and

12

making a new hole in my chest.

"Get rid of him," the doorman growled.

"Let me save you the trouble," I offered. "I can walk out."

"You misunderstood," he replied as he began to smile. "You're not walking anywhere."

Yeah, that tracks.

I waited until Scarecrow took a step. Then I pivoted, slapped the gun sideways just as he squeezed the trigger. The shot went wide, directly into the doorman's knee.

He dropped like a sack of meat and started screaming. Loud. Wet. Red all over.

The Scarecrow stared, frozen at the sight of his friend writhing on the floor. I didn't. I slid behind him and drove my elbow into the base of his skull. He hit the floor, lights out.

I picked up the revolver and checked the cylinder. Still had some teeth.

"You should see a doctor," I told the big guy as I stepped toward him. He was moaning and trying to hold his knee together. I bent over and took my money back.

"I just need to find Metal."

"I don't know where he is," he groaned.

I raised the gun to his other knee and thumbed the hammer back.

"No! Please! Try Louis! He hangs at Comfort Cove!"

"You sure?" I asked pressing the barrel into his good knee. "I'd hate to have to come back."

"Yeah! I'm sure! He's the only one who might know."

That was all I needed.

I dumped the bullets in the bathroom toilet and left the gun in a dumpster outside of the building. No use walking around with a gun that I was pretty sure could be linked to some type of crime. As for Scarecrow and the doorman, they'd live. Maybe. Not my problem.

I made it back to my car and turned toward the Comfort Cove. Something told me things were going to get worse before they got better.

And I was fine with that.

CHAPTER 3

It took me thirty minutes to get to the Comfort Cove. It was the kind of place that didn't just reek of desperation, it marinated in it. A boarded-up dive clinging to the edge of the city like a cancerous wart. Metal would've felt right at home.

The parking lot was half-mud, half-oil slick. Empty beer cans and cigarette butts crunched underfoot. It looked like no one had ever cleaned the place, and anyone who tried probably ended up bleeding behind the dumpster. The front windows were papered with grime. If you could read through the dirt, you'd see a neon sign flickering the word "OPEN," like some cruel joke.

The exterior looked condemned. Inside was worse. Dim, humid and rank. A broken jukebox wheezed out music no one wanted to hear, probably on loop since the Clinton administration. Trash covered the floor like confetti after a funeral. I stepped in and let the door swing shut behind me, cutting off what little light had spilled in. My eyes slowly adjusted. So did the regulars who were blinking like rats caught in the sun.

The clientele was a collection of hard cases. Faces pocked by time and crime, eyes dulled or jittery depending on their drug of choice. This was the kind of place where secrets got traded like poker chips and nobody left with clean hands.

The bartender was a walking tattoo convention with the hygiene of a grease trap. Behind the bar, he eyed me like I was an overdue bill. A man across the room nursed his drink like he owed it child support. Parole fresh. Maybe.

I stepped up to the bar with the dumb grin I used when I wanted people to underestimate me.

"Afternoon."

The bartender grunted. No warmth. No civility. Just meat and suspicion.

"Too early for happy hour?"

He slid a filthy glass toward me and filled it with something gold from a bottle that might've once had a label. It sloshed when he shoved it over. I stared at it like it owed me answers.

"Is this diet?" I asked looking back up at the bartender.

"Does it matter?"

"I'm watching my figure."

That got a twitch in the corner of his mouth. A patron swaggered up beside me, breath thick with rotgut and something worse.

"Who are you?" he asked.

"Who are you?"

He leaned in. His teeth looked like they'd survived a war. "I'm the one asking the questions."

"Well, I'm just the guy regretting this drink." I pointed at his empty glass. "That looked good. I'll have what you're having."

"You couldn't handle what I'm having," he sneered. His pupils were saucers. Wired or fried. Probably both.

"Internet said this place had great reviews."

He blinked.

"You're lying."

"You're right. Lighting's terrible. One star."

He grabbed my shirt, lifted me like I was luggage. I was getting concerned over everyone's ability to pick me up.

"Start talking. Now."

"Alright! I'll tell you where grandma hides the money!"

The punch hit like a freight train. Gut shot. I dropped to my knees, breath stolen. They laughed.

I clawed back up using the bar like a crutch. I spit blood. "I'm looking for Louis," I replied through a gritted smile.

"I'm Louis," the bartender growled.

Perfect. The guy who served me poison was my lead.

"Well, Louis. I'm looking for Metal. I was told you knew where I could find him."

The bartender looked to the bruiser beside me. That didn't bode well.

"You Metal?" I asked with exasperation while turning toward my assaulter.

"What do you want?"

"Just a few questions."

"You a cop?"

"Would it help if I was?"

"Not for you."

"I didn't think so." I leaned in. "I need to ask you about your dead girlfriend."

That stopped him.

"What? She's not dead."

"You didn't know? Died in a car wreck about a week ago."

He froze. Then rage. Not grief. Telling.

"How?"

"A car wreck," I said realizing that he wasn't hearing everything I was saying. "As for the rest of the information, that's what I'm trying to find out."

He stared. "You're lying."

"I'm not."

"Hold him."

Louis grabbed my wrists and slammed them to the bar. Metal made a call, murmured something, and then returned with a smirk.

"She says she's fine." And someone's been harassing her."

"What?" Dead women usually don't answer phone calls. "That doesn't make any sense."

"She also said someone's been harassing her and asking about my business."

Two more guys emerged. One locked the door. Leather vest. Chain. Muscle. The other looked like a string bean with a mean streak.

"Wrong lie to tell, friend."

"Maybe we break his legs," Leather Vest said. "He'll talk."

"Look," I said, calm as I could. "This is all a misunderstanding."

Metal pulled out a switchblade. Flicked it open. Steel flashed.

"I'm a man of principle. I let a lot slide. But not business."

"I can't say I believe either of those statements," I said, bracing myself and quickly trying to think of a way out.

He pressed the blade close to my face. His pupils were pulsing. A cocktail of drugs and ego. Then he flipped the blade and drove it straight through the back of my left hand. The bar caught it. My body screamed. So did I.

"Who are you?!"

Pain blurred everything. Blood soaked the wood. Louis let go of one arm but held the other pinned.

"Tell me or I'll carve you up!"

I acted.

My right fist surged upward between his legs. Hard. Solid. Something cracked. He dropped, shrieking. I yanked my wounded hand up and felt skin tearing as the knife stayed buried. Louis reached for a sawed-off behind the bar. I shattered the dirty glass against his face. Glass and blood flew.

Leather Vest lunged. I spun and slapped him with my impaled hand. Knife first. The blade raked across his cheek, split it open like a zipper. He wailed, falling to the floor and grasping at this face.

I drove a boot into his jaw. He dropped, sliding into a wall like wet laundry. He didn't get back up.

The skinny one panicked. Bolted for the door. Fumbled the lock. Got it open. And disappeared into the light.

I turned. Metal writhed on the floor. I stomped his stomach. He groaned and curled. I yanked the knife out of my hand. Pain shot up my spine and my vision swam. I mounted his chest, knife at his throat. He stopped moving.

"We got off on the wrong foot, Metal."

"I'm not Metal," he croaked.

"What?"

"I didn't say I was. You asked. I didn't answer."

He grinned and laughed. Blood in his teeth. Chaos in his eyes.

I kneed him in the groin again. He arched up, directly into the knife.

"That's sharp," I said, as blood beaded at his throat. "I'm looking for Metal. Tell me where he is or I help you with that smile."

"I don't know where he is. Haven't seen him in days. He's probably at the garage."

"Where?"

He gave it up. An old auto shop in the hills, abandoned but used for everything but cars. Drinking, drugs, debauchery. A den of liars.

"His girlfriend might be there."

"Stephanie?"

"Yeah. Ask her."

So no one knew she was dead. That was interesting.

I slammed the knife into the floor beside his head, grabbed his hair, and drove my knee into his nose. It crunched and he went limp.

Louis moaned behind the bar, face a bloody jigsaw. The shotgun was out of reach. He saw me looking and froze.

I grabbed a towel from off the counter and wrapped my hand. I needed a hospital. I needed answers.

And apparently, I needed to meet Metal in person.

Hopefully, he was more polite than his fan club.

CHAPTER 4

The ER was a lesson in patience and pain. I sat on a gurney for over an hour, watching the fluorescent lights hum like dying insects while a mother screamed into her phone and a guy with a fork in his hand argued about triage. Emergency rooms, turns out, are rarely for emergencies. It's all perspective.

When I finally got called back, a tired physician with the warmth of a grave digger stitched my hand up with all the gentleness of a man darning a sock. Clean cut, straight through. Missed bone and ligaments by inches. Lucky me. The doc didn't say much, but I could tell from the way he squirted antiseptic like he was seasoning a steak that he didn't care for my type.

The hand throbbed. Hot and angry. I flexed it gently, fighting the pain as stitches strained and fire coursed through every tendon. Babying it wasn't an option. Not with what I had coming.

My mind drifted back to the corpse in the canal. Stephanie. Mary swore it wasn't an accident. I didn't believe in coincidences, but I also didn't buy everything that came out of Mary's honey-dipped lips. Something wasn't right, and I needed the truth. Truth had a price.

And it was usually paid in blood, pain, or paperwork. I wasn't much for paperwork. I pulled out my phone and hit the number on speed dial. Three rings.

"It's been a while," the voice said.

"But not too long. You miss me?"

"Only like a rash. What do you want, Deveroux?"

"Nice to hear you too, Mikey."

"The only time you call is when you want something. So let's skip the foreplay."

Mike Jergenson. Mikey. Younger, sharper, still too clean around the edges to know where the real stains were. We'd partnered back when I wore a badge. After I left the department, he'd decided to stick around. Now he was sliding his way up to detective and still answering my calls.

"That car in the ravine. Girl. Solo driver. Ring a bell?"

"You mean the 'accidental non-accident'?"

"That the official title?"

"No, but it should be."

"You running it?"

"Yeah. They think giving me the reins makes me feel special."

"They right?"

"More than you ever were. What do you want?"

"The autopsy. I want to tag along."

"You mean like a 'ride-along'? Are you serious?"

"Yes, Mikey. A field trip. I'll even pack snacks."

"You think this is a joke?"

"No, but I think you're funny when you're flustered."

He sighed so hard I could feel the eye-roll through the receiver.

"Look, I was going after lunch."

"Perfect. I already ate."

"I hate you. Twenty minutes. Don't be late."

I was already leaning against my car when Mikey pulled into the lot. Used suit that he was trying to look new, tie crooked, expression somewhere between "cop mode" and "school principal on a bad day."

"You're early," he said.

"You're late."

"You look like hell."

"You always start with compliments?"

He nodded toward my wrapped hand. "Hospital called in a knife wound. Victim vanished before a squad car showed."

"Sounds reckless."

"Sounds familiar."

"It was a dog," I said holding my bandaged hand up for him to see.

"Four-legged?"

"Two-legged. Big mouth. Knife-shaped teeth."

"Let me guess, you let him go out of kindness?"

"I believe in second chances."

He gave me a long, knowing look. Then shook his head and walked toward the coroner's entrance. "Come on, old man. Let's go see the dead girl."

Dr. Milchin was already waiting inside. White coat. Pale as chalk. Eyes gleaming with childlike glee. If the Joker went to med school and never stopped smiling, you'd get this guy. He rubbed his hands together like he was about to unwrap a birthday gift.

"Detective! Mr. Deveroux! Welcome, welcome! I was just prepping!" He clapped, literally clapped. "You're in for a treat today!"

Mikey looked at me like I owed him ten apologies. I just nodded toward Milchin. "Let the magic begin."

Milchin pulled back the sheet with dramatic flair. "And here she is! Stephanie McCallister. A real mystery wrapped in a charred enigma."

She was burnt badly, face barely recognizable. What hadn't been seared looked pale and bruised. The autopsy incision was a clean zipper down the chest, stitched back like a seamstress' work.

"Pretty girl," Milchin said wistfully.

"Focus, Doc," Mikey replied, arms crossed.

"Right, right! Let's get to the juicy part!" He grabbed a probe like a magician pulling his wand. "So, as you might expect, trauma from the crash was significant. But here's the kicker!" He stabbed the probe under the left breast. It disappeared almost entirely. "She was dead before the car lit up."

Mikey blinked. "Come again?"

"Pre-mortem. As in, already departed. No ticket for the fireball express."

"Cause?"

"Bullet. Nine-millimeter. Ball round. Nothing exotic, nothing poetic. Entered under the rib, bounced around like a pinball and shredded her left lung and heart."

He lifted a kidney dish with a mangled bullet inside. "And voila! Still warm. Kidding! It's actually rather cold."

"You find this at the scene?" I asked.

"Nope! Dug it out myself, right here in the chest cavity. Like treasure hunting."

"There were no casings at the scene," Mikey muttered.

"Which means she was shot elsewhere," I added. "Dumped. Burned to hide the truth."

"Our accident just became a homicide," Mikey said.

"Gold star for the detective," I muttered.

"You want to take over the case?" he shot back.

"Only if you promise to cry about it."

"Bite me."

"Later. I have stitches."

Milchin clapped again. "Isn't this fun? You boys should come more often! I have one in the other room that forgot to strap in on a roller coaster!"

"We'll bring popcorn," Mikey grunted.

I turned to leave. "Thanks for the corpse tour, Doc. Always a pleasure."

Milchin beamed. "Anytime! Don't be strangers!"

Back in the hallway, Mikey slowed his stride.

"So?" Mikey asked, letting the question hang for a moment.

"So your victim was murdered. Your scene was staged. And Mary might not be as clueless as she acts."

"That woman is a walking red flag."

"Yeah. But she hired me. And she wants answers."

"You think she lied to me? You think she lied to you?"

"I think everyone does. Eventually."

He shook his head. "I liked this case better when it was open and shut."

"Then you're in the wrong city, Mikey."

He sighed, but there was no real fight in it. Just worry.

"Be careful, Steve."

"Always. Until I'm not."

I left with my hand burning, my head buzzing, and one truth finally unwrapped: Stephanie McCallister didn't die by accident.

Someone killed her.

And I was going to find out why.

CHAPTER 5

After a gas station coffee that tasted like regret and a minute to cool down, I figured it was time to check in with Mary. Not just for the case. She had one of those faces that made you forget why you were mad in the first place, and I hadn't looked at anything that pretty since I walked past a bakery at 3 a.m.

She answered on the first ring and said she could meet me on her break. She worked at a clothing store downtown. What she didn't mention was that it was the kind of place that sold more lace than logic.

I walked in and stopped cold. Lace, silk, red lights, and estrogen. Lingerie. And me, the only man in sight. Every head turned. I wasn't a detective anymore. I was a pervert under fluorescent lighting.

A woman near me took a half-step back.

"Just looking for a dressing room," I said with my best innocent smile. She backed away like I was contagious. "You're too old for this stuff anyway, grandma," I muttered.

Then Mary appeared, all curves and confidence, with that smile that could raise blood pressure and legal questions. Her hair was pulled back just enough to showcase a neckline that didn't ask for attention but received it anyway. She moved with a grace that wasn't for show, it was habit. She didn't strut or slink. She simply existed in the room like gravity bent toward her.

"Glad you made it," she said, her voice soft and warm, a velvet echo.

"Apparently you're the only one," I said, nodding toward the rest of the crowd still trying to figure out if I was security or a stalker.

She glanced at my hand and the smile flickered. "Are you okay?"

"Just a little mishap. Bad run-in with some... faulty tools."

She took my hand gently. Her touch was soft, warm. Dangerous. "Come on. We can talk in the back."

We slipped into the employee break room, a dingy little space with a coffee maker older than my moral compass. I straightened my shirt, as if that would help.

I gave her the censored version of the bar brawl minus the blood, bruises, and body count. Her eyes narrowed when I described one of the men.

"I know him," she said her voice soft and heavy.

"That right?"

She hesitated, then sank into the chair across from me. She didn't speak right away, and when she did, her voice dropped an octave, like she was unearthing a secret she'd buried deep.

"He used to come around with Metal. He tried to be charming which lasted about five minutes. He said the right things, wore the right clothes, but there was something about his eyes. They were cold. Like he was watching people the way a butcher sizes up livestock."

I leaned in. "Go on."

"He started texting me, calling me, showing up where I worked. I told him I wasn't interested, but he didn't hear no. He started spreading rumors that we were together. Told people I was his girl. It was like he was rewriting reality and expecting me to play along."

She looked down, her hands fidgeting now. There was something fragile in the way she folded them together, like she was trying to hold herself together too.

"The worst part was, I started seeing signs. He had money that didn't make sense. Conversations that stopped when I entered the room. People looked scared of him. I think he was running with someone or something. Gangs. Drug dealers. I never had proof and whenever I asked about it he always had a story that didn't quite add up."

I didn't interrupt. Her voice had gone flat, emotion stuffed behind years of trying to stay safe.

"One night, I woke up and he was outside my building. Just standing there. Smoking. Watching. I called the cops. They said unless he came in, there was nothing they could do. That's when I got the restraining order. It didn't stop him, though. It just made him sneakier."

"You did the right thing. Guy like that, you don't play nice."

She gave me a look. One part gratitude, two parts something else.

"You going to talk to him?"

"That's the plan."

"Be careful. I think he enjoys violence."

She placed her hands on mine. My pulse skipped like a scratched record.

"I don't want you to get hurt."

That one landed harder than it should have. Maybe it was the bandages. Maybe it was the way she said "you."

"I can take care of myself."

"That's not the same as not getting hurt."

"I'll be fine," I lied smoothly, with a smile. Because that's what you do when the beautiful woman looking at you like you matter is also the one handing you the loaded gun.

She brushed a strand of hair behind her ear. The move was so practiced, so natural, it felt weaponized. "I should get back. Don't want to give people the wrong idea."

Would that really be so bad?

"Right. Wouldn't want to damage my reputation in front of the bras and panties."

"Stop by after work?" she asked, pausing at the door. "Just to make sure I get home okay."

"Sure. It's what professionals do."

We both knew I was lying. But we both liked the sound of it.

She gave me one last look over her shoulder. Smile soft. Eyes full of questions. Then she vanished through the curtain of lace and neon.

I stared at the door a little too long.

Real men don't get butterflies.

Another lie I kept telling myself.

CHAPTER 6

The road curled through the canyon like a coiled snake. Quiet, patient, and ready to strike. I rolled slow, hand resting on the wheel while the other was gripping a dull ache where Bolt's goon had introduced me to his fist earlier. My ribs weren't broken, but they were writing a strongly worded letter to my spine.

The autopsy hadn't given me any answers, just more shadows to chase. Stephanie didn't kill herself that much was clear. What wasn't clear was who had. And why. Metal was the obvious suspect, but obvious usually means someone's laying breadcrumbs in the wrong direction.

I knew Mikey. By now, he'd be back at the precinct lining up evidence like toy soldiers, probably warming up the SWAT van just in case I stirred the wrong hornet's nest. Which meant I had to get ahead of him fast.

Metal's garage sat at the far end of nowhere, draped in rust and neglect. An old gas station joined to a boarded-up general store, the kind of place that died screaming in the '80s and nobody came back to check the body.

The only thing that looked alive was a Mustang Fastback parked out front, polished like a mirror at a mob funeral. That told me someone still cared. Probably Metal. Or someone with worse taste and more bullets.

I parked down the hill and walked in quietly. The place was silent, but not the kind of peaceful that puts you at ease. The kind that gets people killed.

The security cameras blinked at me from both corners of the building as I approached. Great. Smile for the dead man's highlight reel.

I stopped and leaned on the Mustang leaving a greasy hand-print right on the driver's side door. Anyone watching would know I wasn't being subtle. I gave it a few beats. Nothing moved. Nothing barked. No welcome committee. After a few minutes of silence, I decided to test fate's door.

The garage door was unlocked. Either someone was sloppy or it was a trap. With my luck, it was the latter. I reached into my pocket and pulled on a pair of gloves. Latex. Unfashionable but sensible. I pushed the door slightly ajar with my foot and slipped inside allowing let the dark swallow me.

The garage was wide, open, and smelled like metal, mildew, and quiet violence. Tools littered the place like forgotten sins, and a Cadillac sat jacked up in the middle of the room big, black, and ominous. The kind of car that never meant good news. I slowly moved along the wall, silent as guilt.

The office was a fishbowl in the back lined with glass windows offering fake privacy. I stole a glance through the open door. Metal was in there, slouched in the boss's chair. Lifeless. His chest was riddled with holes, dried blood mapping a Jackson Pollock down his shirt. The stench in the room hit me like a sucker punch. He'd been marinating for days. No AC. No airflow. Just rot and regret.

I searched him first. His pockets were empty. His wallet gone. No phone and no keys. No answers.

The office didn't help. There was no laptop and no papers. A drawer full of syringes and a little white powder. Junkie gear and empty bottles were everywhere but not much else. The only other room, housing the camera gear, was stripped clean. No footage. No clues.

Whoever did this took their time. They knew what they wanted and had left nothing behind but questions and rot.

Then came the screech of tires.

I ducked behind a tool bench just as two sets of boots pounded through the garage door. I recognized one of them by the scar I gave him back at Comfort Cove. The other guy had run out of the bar when everything kicked off.

They found Metal fast. Scarface stepped into the office, took one whiff, and lost his lunch on the floor.

"Damn," I whispered. "Even your stomach knows you're not built for this."

I shifted along the far wall trying to sneak out as quietly as possible. I made it halfway around the Cadillac before a shadow blocked my path.

Bolt.

His face hadn't changed. Same dead eyes, same cracked smile. But now he had a cannon of a revolver aimed at my chest.

"Hi again," I said with a smile I didn't mean. "How've you been?"

He wasn't in a talking mood. "I've been better," he said, cocking the hammer.

Then a voice called out: "Bolt! Metal's dead! You better come see this."

Bolt. Scarface. Metal. These guys picked their names from a toolbox and their morals from the trash. He yanked me upright and shoved me through the door like a bad delivery.

Scarface saw me and flinched like I was the ghost of bar fights past.

"Thanks for checking the room so thoroughly," Bolt growled.

Scarface mumbled something and looked away. Guilt? Embarrassment? Didn't matter. I wasn't going to live long enough to psychoanalyze.

"You kill him?" he asked, still pointing the cannon at me.

"No. I was gonna ask him a few questions. That turned out to be a dead end."

That earned me a punch. Kidney again. My body folded like a cheap cot. He grabbed my injured hand and twisted. I screamed. He twisted harder. My stitches ripped.

"You want to walk out of here?" he said.

"That a real option?" I was able to choke out while trying not to pass out from the pain.

He squeezed harder. "Start talking."

"Alright. Metal owed me money. I came to collect." Blood began to run down my wrist and into my jacket sleeve.

"Liar."

"Okay. I was hoping for a Groupon." He punched again in the same spot. That kidney was going to file for divorce.

"Why are you here?" he screamed.

"Looking for answers. Stephanie's dead. I thought he might know something."

He paused. The name meant something. Maybe more.

"You talk to her?" I felt his grip on my hand release and he took a step back, staring down on me as I breathed heavily and sweat profusely.

"Not recently," I said looking up at him.

Scarface glanced between us. "This guy's a cop."

"Not anymore," I muttered, cradling my hand. "I just have boundary issues."

Bolt raised the revolver again and jammed it under my chin. "You think this is a game?"

"I'm not much into games," I responded desperately trying to regain my composure.

Scarface stepped forward. "What if he's telling the truth?"

"He's not."

"What if he is?" Scarface protested.

Bolt didn't like being questioned. He turned his attention to Scarface and I saw my opening. I lunged forward, swung my arm under his and yanked the revolver sideways. It fired, deafening, into the wall. I rammed my knee up into his groin again. The man had no luck there. He dropped. I snatched the gun, burst out of the office and dove for cover behind the car.

"You're not walking out of here!" he screamed while holding his crotch, fury spitting with every syllable.

"Yeah," I said, aiming back at the open office door, daring someone to step out. "You keep saying that."

He pulled out another gun. I ducked as he fired wildly, missing his mark while his two lackeys drew their own guns.

More gunshots rang out. Scarface fired blind through the office windows. I returned fire and he went down in a spray of red and silence.

That left Bolt and one last goon. The kid looked shaken, scared. Bolt didn't care. He screamed orders and threats at the skinny man. Then he lit something. Molotov. Old school.

He lit it and hurled it out of the office. He was a terrible shot. He missed and the bottle shattered across the room. Flames exploded against the wall, licking up the paint, feeding on the oil-stained concrete. Smoke followed and I stayed low, my vision blurring. The heat began rapidly rising.

The first bottle missed but the second didn't. It landed in a bucket of rags close to me. Flames caught the oil-streaked clothe like they'd been waiting for it. Smoke filled the air. The garage had turned into an oven that was going to cook us alive.

Bolt screamed at his last goon to throw another. The kid hesitated.

"Light it!"

"I can't see him!" the kid protested.

"Light it!" Bolt pointed his revolver at the strung out goon who was shaking from fear, withdrawals or adrenaline. Possibly all three.

"I don't want to die!"

"You will if you don't!"

Gunshot.

Bolt executed his own guy. Smoke. Flame. Rage.

Then silence.

"You and me now!" he roared, turning back towards where he had thrown the two bottles. "Come on! Be a man!" Heavy smoke was filling the garage like a heavy blanket smothering light and sucking out the oxygen. He ventured out trying to find his next kill.

I made my move.

Diving behind the Cadillac, I gripped and raised the revolver. I stayed low to the ground and watched his footsteps as he walked past me. Crouching, I moved behind him and stood up, pointing the revolver directly at him. One hand shaky, one hand steady.

"You said it was just us," I told him. "You were right."

He spun. I pulled the trigger.

Bolt's head jerked forward as the bullet entered his forehead and removed every thought he had. He dropped, still wearing that same half-smirk.

Smoke choked the room as the flames danced too close.

I moved fast, grabbing the phone from Bolt's coat and dialed 911.

"Help! He's trying to kill me!" I fired three rounds into the wall for good measure, then dropped the phone and revolver into the flames. As I stepped outside, I made one last stop at the Mustang.

I pulled out a rag and wiped the door clean of my prints. No sense getting sloppy now.

I walked into the smoky dusk, one step ahead of the fire, one step behind the truth.

CHAPTER 7

I stopped at a diner on the edge of town. It was the kind of place where the seats stuck to your legs and the coffee came with a side of existential crisis. I ordered pancakes because dinner was too complicated and I needed something soft enough to cut through with a busted hand.

The syrup helped slow my heartbeat. Adrenaline withdrawal does weird things to your body. It makes you shaky and makes your brain go full static. I stared at my plate like it might offer closure. It didn't. It just got cold.

The blood had soaked through my bandage again. I'd need to deal with that before the smell started drawing attention. I pulled out my phone and left a voicemail for Mary. Just the basics. Her boyfriend was dead. I left out the part where the garage lit up like a Fourth of July barbecue and bodies dropped like confetti.

She didn't need that kind of color commentary.

She called back just as the waitress dropped off the check. I told her I needed to look at Stephanie's car. Mary said it was still in the impound lot. She gave me the address and I promised to keep her updated, then hung up.

The impound lot was closed by the time I got there. A rusted chain-link fence wrapped around the place like a bad conscience. There were two cameras. One at the gate and the other watching the office. Nothing on the lot's backside but shadows and bad intentions.

I circled the perimeter, found the darkest corner, and tested the fence. No dogs barked. No guards yelled. Just me and a flashlight I hoped didn't flicker when I needed it.

Up and over.

The lot was a museum of mechanical regret. Wrecked, burned, broken or impounded. Rows of history nobody wanted. Stephanie's yellow sedan stood out like a sore thumb that'd been set on fire. The back half was charred. The blackened metal curling like paper. But the front seats? Barely touched.

Which didn't make sense.

If she'd been in the driver's seat, she'd have been roasted unevenly. But her body was burned head to toe. Except for her face and shoulders. It was like someone had propped her up in the backseat after the fire started. Or possibly before.

There were no bullet holes in the seatbacks. No blood spray. No broken glass that didn't belong. This wasn't panic, it was planning. Someone staged this. They'd taken their time and cleaned up after. They had left nothing but char and confusion.

I popped the passenger door and started sifting through the wreckage. Stephanie wasn't a neat freak. The front floorboard was a landfill of receipts, takeout bags, and wristbands. Lots of wristbands. All from the same place. The Last Point. Real subtle branding. My money was on glow sticks and bad decisions.

My phone buzzed again. I cursed and fumbled to silence it, but it was too late. It rang loud enough to wake the dead.

I answered in a whisper. "Yeah?"

"Why are you whispering?" Mikey's voice came through.

"I'm... at a theater."

"You're answering during the movie? That seems a bit inconsiderate."

"You called me, Mikey."

"I figured you'd be ignoring me like usual, so I was going to leave a message. You still working the McCallister case?

"Until something more lucrative walks through the door," I replied while rifling through the contents on the floorboard.

He hesitated. That meant it was good.

"I shouldn't be calling you. This stays between us."

"Of course," I said, knowing full well there was nobody I could talk to about the case even if I wanted to.

"We got a search warrant for the boyfriend's place. Shawn Taylor. AKA Metal."

I'd already made the visit but I didn't say that. "We found drugs. Stolen goods. A rifle."

"Same caliber as the one that killed Stephanie?" I asked.

"No. Rifle's unrelated. But here's the thing, we got a call about a shooting out near the canyon while we were still searching. A garage was on fire and four bodies were found. One of them was Metal."

I let out a low whistle. "Yikes. Was he charging too much for spark

41

plugs?"

"I feel like I might be telling you something you already know."

I shrugged, forgetting he couldn't see it. "Not at all. Just no surprised is all."

Mikey didn't bite. "We found a phone at the scene. Half-melted, but traceable. It belonged to a guy named Gerald Davis. Street name's Bolt."

I barked out a laugh. "No. No, no, no. You're telling me Bolt's real name is Gerald? That's amazing. These guys sound like they met during a failed boy band audition."

"Yeah, well, they're both dead now," Mikey replied. "The fire's still under investigation. But here's the part that smells funny—someone called it in from that phone. Seconds before it burned."

"Coincidence?"

"Sure. And I'm secretly the Queen of Denmark." There was a beat of silence. Then his voice dropped into cop-mode. "You didn't happen to be anywhere near that garage, did you?"

I cleared my throat. "I thought you said this was off the record?"

"I did. But my gut says otherwise."

"Your gut also once said the vending machine egg salad was a good idea."

"Deveroux."

"Mikey."

"Just tell me whether or not you're a suspect in all of this."

"I'm not the bad guy. Does that work?"

He sighed, long and slow. "I'm checking out the impound lot tomorrow. Want to meet me?"

I glanced at the burnt-out car then pulled the wristbands into my coat pocket.

"Yeah. See you in the morning."

"Try not to start any more fires, okay?"

"No promises."

He hung up. I climbed back over the fence and disappeared into the shadows, still bleeding, still hunted, still asking the wrong questions.

But I was getting close.

And that scared me more than it should have.

CHAPTER 8

I pulled up to the curb outside Mary's work just as the neon flickered in the display window behind her. She stood beneath the buzzing sign like something out of a dream wrapped in soft fabric and bad timing. Legs for days, a dress that made gravity feel like a flirtation, and a look on her face that made me question every good decision I'd ever made.

Before I could even kill the engine, she opened the passenger door and slid in, crossing her legs like she'd practiced it in front of a jury.

"I was starting to think you stood me up," she said, her smile just shy of dangerous.

"If this were a date," I replied, "you'd have grounds to sue."

"If this were a date," she said, smoothing the hem of her dress, "you'd have worn a cleaner shirt."

I didn't argue. I just pulled away from the curb and merged into traffic like a man driving off a cliff.

"What did you find out?" she asked, her eyes were on me like she already knew I wasn't going to tell her everything.

"That your friend had a talent for picking the wrong men," I said. "Metal was a fire hazard in human skin. And his buddy, Bolt made Metal look like a service puppy."

She didn't flinch. "He once broke a pool stick over a guy's back for not playing fast enough."

"Sounds about right," I muttered.

She gave me directions to her place. I filed them away like I didn't already look her up two days ago.

"Mind if I ask you something about Stephanie?" I said.

She glanced over, guarded.

"Depends what kind of question."

"The kind you're not gonna like." I waited a beat. "Was she using? Drugs?"

Her jaw tightened. "No. She wouldn't touch that stuff."

"Her boyfriend did."

"I know. But she wasn't like that."

"She lived with it," I said. "People get pulled into worse things for less."

Mary looked down at her hands, then at me. "She tried to get him to quit. But he'd get angry. It got ugly. She told me he scared her sometimes, but she was stuck. He wouldn't let her go."

She reached across the console, her fingers brushing mine. Her touch was light, warm and intentional.

"She was good, Steve. Don't let the way she died define who she was."

I wanted to believe her. But belief was expensive, and I was running on credit.

"I need the truth," I said. "Not what you might hope to be true."

"She didn't use," she said again, voice trembling on the edge of defiance.

I didn't press her. Not yet.

Twenty minutes later, we pulled up to her building. It was one of those upscale high-rises with security cameras and flowerbeds that cost more than my rent. The kind of place that whispers "money" without ever raising its voice.

"This is... nice," I said.

"It does the job," she replied.

"Lingerie must pay better than I thought."

She smirked. "Who says that's my only job?"

I looked at her, really looked at her. There were layers. None of them safe.

"What else do you work hard on?" I asked, already regretting the question.

She leaned in, lips near my ear, voice soft as sin. "Anything that excites me."

I swallowed hard, counted to five, then again.

She reclined in her seat, letting the streetlight wash across her collarbones like a spotlight designed by temptation itself. My pulse tapped out Morse code on my ribs.

"You find the car?" she asked, as if nothing was happening.

"Yeah. Burned out but still talking. I'll be digging more in the morning."

"So you're done working tonight?" she asked letting the side of her mouth turn up into a smile.

"Not unless you've got a fresh murder I should know about."

"No murders. Just a conversation... maybe a drink... upstairs."

Her voice was silk, the tone of her suggestion seemed dipped in honey. Every nerve in my body was screaming say yes, but my brain, what was left of it, reminded me that crossing lines had a way of making corpses out of men like me.

I turned to her. "I'd love to."

Her smile told me she knew what was coming.

"But I can't. Not yet. Not while I'm still working this."

"Professional boundaries?" she asked, raising a brow.

"Something like that."

She nodded, slowly. "Rain check, then."

She leaned in close, her breath was warm on my cheek. "Now you know where I live," she whispered, lips just brushing my ear.

I froze. Couldn't move. Didn't want to.

Then she was gone. Door open, heels on pavement, hips swaying like punctuation marks on a sentence I'd never get to finish.

"Thanks for the ride," she called back, looking over her shoulder.

And just like that, the night swallowed her whole.

I sat there a moment too long. Then I drove off.

Back   into   the   dark.   Alone.   Again.

CHAPTER 9

The sun was trying to convince the city it had good intentions when I pulled into the impound yard at nine sharp. Mikey was already there, leaning against his car with a cup of bad coffee and worse posture.

"You drink yet?" he asked, like it was a moral check.

"I had orange juice."

"Orange juice?" He raised an eyebrow. "Real men drink coffee."

"Real men don't care what other men drink."

"Touché." He sipped his sludge and led the way through the gate.

Stephanie's car looked worse in the daylight. Charred like a memory no one wanted to keep. Mikey made a beeline straight to the car.

"You know exactly where it is?" I asked, a bit accusingly as if he'd already been here before. Like the pot calling the kettle black.

"I asked the front desk. You should try it sometime."

"Sounds dangerously close to logic."

He popped open the driver's door and started digging. "You want to help or just look pretty?"

"You've clearly got the pretty part covered," I said, circling to the passenger side.

I'd been here once already, but night and adrenaline had a way of distorting details. This time, I took my time and Mikey was still able to quickly come to the same conclusion I did.

"Look at this," he said, holding up a wristband. "The Last Point. Think she was a regular?"

"About as regular as you and caffeine addiction."

"You're saying she went every day?"

"You're getting better at this, Mikey. I'm beginning to be proud of you."

The club had security cameras. I remembered them from the last time I got threatened in a place with more neon than class. If she was there the night she died, maybe someone had footage.

"You thinking of checking it out?" I asked.

"Yeah, but somehow I get the feeling you already knew that."

"You'll need someone with you. Someone charming. Rugged. Handsome."

"Two of me?" I walked right into that one and couldn't decide how to respond. After a moment of me staring blankly back at him, he sighed. "You volunteering?"

"Well I do happen to be between beatings at the moment."

"Just so you know," Mikey said, eyeing my wrinkled shirt, "you're wearing the same thing as yesterday."

"Laundry's overrated."

He sniffed and recoiled. "So's deodorant and a shower, apparently."

We agreed to hit the club that afternoon. In the meantime, I asked about the ravine where they'd found Stephanie's car.

"You remember the garage shooting I told you about?" Mikey asked.

"Hard to forget."

"I'm sure it is," he replied giving me a knowing look. "That ravine's about fifteen minutes from there. On foot."

My brain did the math. Metal's garage. Stephanie's torched car. Fifteen minutes apart.

I didn't believe in coincidences. I believed in patterns.

A few hours later we found ourselves at The Last Point. The club was open but quiet. A skeleton staff was prepping for the night's sins. Mikey went in first and I followed, feeling déjà vu tingle up my spine.

A bartender looked up from restocking. He was tall, athletic and in his mid-twenties. One of those frat-boy lifers who thought charisma was a personality.

"We're not open," he called.

I recognized him. He looked up and recollection sunk into his demeanor. The last time I saw him, he was half-running out of Metal's place with panic in his eyes.

"Funny," I said. "We keep running into each other."

Mikey looked between us. "You two know each other?"

"No," the bartender lied with the confidence of a man who thinks lies can be recycled.

Mikey showed his badge. "We've got questions."

"Of course you do." The bartender tried to play it cool, but his hands fumbled with a bottle. I'd seen steadier hands on drunks.

"What's your name?" Mikey asked.

"David."

"David what?" I added.

"Collins."

"Do you know Stephanie McCallister? Or Metal?"

"Everyone knows Metal," David muttered, bitterness baked into every word.

"You two have issues?" I asked, watching his body language.

"Everyone had issues with Metal. He thought he was king of the sewer rats."

"So you knew him."

"I didn't say that."

"But you know where he lived, right?"

"No idea," he replied, attempting to keep busy with his stocking duties. That lie had a limp.

Mikey pushed. "What about Stephanie?"

"She was too good for him. He treated her like garbage. He was controlling and he would yell at her in public. Made her sit while he held court with dealers and wannabes."

"So you knew her well?"

"No," he said quickly. Too quickly.

Mikey and I exchanged a look. One we'd shared a hundred times. This guy was hiding something. Probably a few things.

Then the owner walked in. He was a short man with a goatee, a belly, and a wardrobe that screamed "midlife crisis meets discount cigar bar."

"I'm the owner," he said. "What's this about?"

"Two of your patrons," Mikey replied showing his badge, "left hear a few days ago. They're both dead."

That got his attention. He invited us back and we followed him into his office. It had an oak desk, fake prestige and several photos with nobodies pretending to be somebodies. The man was a local legend in his own mind.

"Stephanie McCallister," Mikey said. "You knew her?"

His face went pale. "She's dead? When?"

"You tell us," I said.

"She was sweet. Everyone liked her." He slumped into his chair letting his eyes wander back and forth across the floor like they were sweeping for comfort.

"What about Metal?" I asked.

"Psychopath. He'd come in, pick fights and act like he owned the place. I had to throw him out more than once and not for being drunk either. The guy was wired even when he was supposedly sober."

"You think he hurt her?" I asked.

"I wouldn't be surprised."

"He's dead too," Mikey said.

The owner sat back, trying to process it all.

"Anyone else want them gone?" I asked.

"Everyone wanted Metal gone. Stephanie? She didn't have enemies."

"When was the last time you saw them?" Mikey asked.

"A week ago."

I stiffened. "David told us it'd been weeks."

The owner scoffed. "Nope. That night, Metal dragged her out into the parking lot.

David went after them. He said he saw Metal getting violent."

"Did he call the cops?"

"He said he did. Said he spent the night giving a statement. Left us short-staffed."

I was starting to like David less and less.

"Do you have security footage from that night?" I asked.

He did.

We watched. No audio, just image. Inside the club: Stephanie and Metal arguing,

David approaching, Metal shoving him. Outside: Metal yelling, grabbing her. David stepping in. Punches were thrown with David getting worked like a speed bag. Metal shoved Stephanie into her car and then they drove off. David waited. Then left in a different vehicle.

It was all there. And none of it matched what David had said.

Mikey asked for a copy and the owner handed him a disc.

We headed back to the main floor. The bar was empty.

"He's gone," Mikey muttered.

"Thank you, Captain Obvious."

Mikey gave me a look.

"Sorry. I forgot, you're not a captain."

He ignored the jab. "David's a suspect now."

"No kidding. You check the statement he filed?"

Mikey nodded grimly. "There wasn't one."

Figures.

The guy lied. He covered up a beating and knew more than he let on.

And   now   he   was   gone.

CHAPTER 10

Mikey and I parted ways not long after the club. I told him to try for a warrant to search David's place. He tried but the judge declined stating there wasn't enough probable cause.

Apparently, being a liar and a walking red flag doesn't cut it in court. Go figure.

David had a few bruises on his record. Traffic tickets. Two alcohol incidents. An assault charge from college that probably involved cheap beer and dumber friends. Nothing capital, but enough to make me trust him less than a politician with a hug.

So I decided to stop being a sidekick and start playing detective again.

I found his apartment easy enough and parked across the street. For twenty minutes, I watched a parking lot full of forgettable cars and realized I had no clue what David drove or if he even had a car. The night he left the club parking lot could've been in anything.

So I played the only card I had left. I walked to knock on his door.

Just as I turned the corner at the top of the stairs, the door opened. And there he was, David Collins, freshly showered and halfway out the door. We locked eyes. His face drained like a guilty kid caught mid-cookie jar.

"Hi, David," I said, all casual venom. "Just a few more questions."

"How the hell did you find me?"

"Google's a beautiful thing. Did you know you have three unpaid parking tickets?"

He bolted.

"David!" I shouted. "I hate running!"

But I ran anyway.

He tore across the street, darting through traffic like his pants were literally on fire. Cars screeched. Horns blared. I zigzagged behind him, close enough to curse him but not close enough to catch.

He veered into a narrow alley, knocking trash bins over behind him which slowed down my already pathetic run time. One metal can clanged hard against my shin and almost cost me my balance. The alley twisted behind a row of crumbling buildings and dead air vents. He jumped a pile of pallets and slammed an old door open into a boiler room. I followed, nearly eating brick.

Through the boiler room. Through a busted hallway that stank of wet drywall and regret. He shoved a mop bucket behind him. I kicked it aside, slipped but recovered before I became a fixture in the wall.

Another alley. Another fence.

This time, he scaled a dumpster then used a broken railing to leap onto a fire escape and climbed like a cat in a panic.

I followed halfway, slipped again and hit the pavement like a bad decision.

By the time I pulled myself up, he was gone. He'd turned a corner and vanished into the city like smoke from a wet cigarette.

I stumbled back across the street, my lungs aching, pride limping. If anyone saw me doubled over and gasping, I hoped they thought I was having a moment of deep reflection instead of a mild cardiac event.

When I caught my breath, I walked up to his apartment and knocked. I wasn't sure if he had a roommate or anyone else was inside. There was no answer. No surprises. I checked the knob. Locked. Again, no surprise.

I pulled out a lock pick set I'd gotten as partial payment from a broke locksmith last fall. Thought it was poetic justice. Only problem was I never learned to use it.

After a few minutes of fumbling, I shoved it back in my coat and circled to the back. Luckily for me it was a ground-level apartment with a very questionable patio door.

I didn't even try finesse this time. One good kick next to the latch and the frame cracked like cheap eggshell. The whole thing popped open. No security bar, no reinforcement. David probably thought he didn't need it. Most men don't think they need security until someone kicks their door in.

I stepped inside.

The place smelled like gym socks, energy drinks, and broken dreams. Dirty dishes were piled in the sink. Empty water bottles and pizza boxes colonized the coffee table. A giant TV dominated the wall, flanked by a stereo system powerful enough to rupture windows and the patience of neighbors. A stack of magazines on the counter suggested David was either learning to bartend better or trying to impress girls who liked men who pretended they read.

I ransacked the place. Or at least did my best make it look worse than it already was. There was no gun. No bloody clothes. No note confessing to murder.

Then I opened the bedroom closet.

And there it was. Crazy.

The walls were covered in photos of Stephanie. Polaroids. Cell phone shots. Selfies she didn't know she'd taken. Some of her clothes were folded neatly on a shelf like he was running a shrine. I didn't like how that felt in my stomach. It wasn't guilt, it was something colder.

I checked the mattress. Nothing under it. But something was in it. Between the mattress and the box spring, I found a videotape.

A literal VHS.

I held it up and stared at it like it might bite me. It was either nothing or everything.

I left the way I came, through the busted patio door and headed to the one place I knew had a working VCR: Gary Donovan's office.

Gary's office looked like it had given up before it ever opened. Beige walls that were yellowed with time and failure. Fluorescent lights buzzed like dying flies. The carpet smelled like damp ashtrays. A fan rotated in the corner, even though it didn't actually push any air.

The receptionist desk was unmanned, as usual. A half-eaten sandwich lay there from the day before, right next to a cracked mug that read World's Okayest Lawyer. On the wall, his law degree hung slightly crooked, probably ashamed of itself.

Gary wasn't in. Lucky him.

I closed the door to the inner office, shoved the tape into the dusty old

VCR he used for divorce depositions back in the day, and hit play.

The screen flared to life in static.

Then: Metal. Standing outside his garage. Angry.

Stephanie. Crying. Pleading.

David appeared on-screen and stepped between them. Metal shoved him then pulled a gun. Stephanie grabbed Metal's arm. He struck her and she dropped hard.

David lunged at Metal. They wrestled.

Stephanie began to stand when the gun went off. She crumpled.

The struggle stopped. David held the weapon. He looked between her and Metal, panicked. Metal stepped forward. David lifted the gun and fired. Again. Again. Until Metal folded like trash.

Then David stood there. Just... stood.

Finally, he dragged Metal's body into the garage. Propped him in the chair. Wiped his face. Found the surveillance system and pulled the tape.

The screen went black.

I sat there, watching the blank screen reflect my face back at me. The tape was raw, ugly, and damning. It was everything.

Only one thing was missing: the gun.

Either he still had it, or it was buried somewhere far away.

And if I knew David, and I was starting to, he'd be trying to disappear by now. But not before he got his hands on some cash. Bartenders didn't get severance packages. They got tips. And tonight, he'd probably come crawling back to the club one last time.

I grabbed my phone and dialed Mikey.

"It's Steve," I said. "I've got something. I need backup."

Mayhem

CHAPTER 11

It was late. Not club-late, for them the party was just starting. For me, it was the hour when you ask yourself hard questions in the mirror or decide to buy a kitchen knife off the shopping channel that claims it can cut through a boot and a tomato with equal ease. I parked a block down from The Last Point and waited.

My watch read 10:45. Mikey had already texted and let me know he was in position out back. He wasn't thrilled with my plan. Said it was reckless. I hadn't shown him the tape. I knew he'd never play along if I had. He'd just slap cuffs on David and pray for a clean confession in a metal chair under a flickering light. That should have been it. I had a feeling there was something else going on that I hadn't found yet. Something else Stephanie was tied into.

I needed the gun. I needed him to talk.

I stepped into the club with the rest of the night crawlers. Inside, the air pulsed with bass and bad perfume. The lights flickered like emergency strobes. The dance floor was a mess of limbs and heat. People moved like they'd been freed from gravity and taste.

I spotted David behind the bar, pouring drinks like they were his last salvation. His eyes were sharp, focused and his hands were quick. He was working for one thing: tips. And a fast exit.

I slid up and dropped a few bills on the counter. "Cranberry juice."

He froze. Eyes on me. Heart probably jackhammering behind his ribs. I could see it, the fight-or-flight response lighting up behind his pupils.

"Don't," I said flatly. "I've got the tape, David. You run again, this gets worse."

He stared. Thought about his options then slowly nodded.

"We need to talk. Out back. Now."

"Who else is out there?" he asked looking back and forth between me and the hallway leading to the back of the club.

"You're mother, genius. Shockingly, you're not living up to her expectations."

"What?" A look of confusion on his face.

"Stop wasting time," I replied. "Let's go."

I turned and walked through the crowd, threading through bodies slick with sweat and desperation. I slipped through the rear exit and waited by the dumpsters. David showed up a minute later, nervous as a fox in a slaughterhouse.

"What do you want?" he asked, voice tight.

"You know what I want."

He glanced around like a man checking for escape hatches. "I didn't kill her."

"Yes, you did."

"No," he barked. "Metal killed her. I tried to stop him."

"I saw the tape, David. All of it. You shot her. Maybe by accident. But you killed Metal on purpose."

His voice cracked. "She told me he was going to hurt her. She begged me to help."

"You didn't even know her."

"I did!" he snapped. "We were in love. She told me. She said he wouldn't let her go."

He started pacing, hands jittering at his sides. His face twisted, warped by grief and guilt.

"You loved her," I said. "So you put her in a car and set it on fire?"

That landed like a slap. He blinked back tears, lip trembling. "I didn't mean to... I panicked."

"You drove the car into the ravine. You set the fire."

"I didn't want to," he said. "She was already gone. I didn't want to leave her there lying on the ground like that."

He was unraveling. And fast.

"David... who told you she was scared? That she loved you?"

He hesitated.

"She told me," he whispered. "She said she needed me. She said I was the only one who could save her."

He wasn't talking to me anymore. He was reciting gospel from inside his own broken brain.

"She said I had to stop him. That only I could. She needed me. And then she was dead. She made me do it."

"She made you?" I stepped closer. "David, listen to yourself..."

"She made me!" he screamed. "Both of them! I couldn't stop either of them!"

His face twisted in rage. His hands trembled. "You showed the tape to the police?"

"Maybe," I lied. "But it doesn't matter because they don't need it. They've got the gun."

He paused. His eyes narrowed.

"No they don't." He lifted his shirt and pulled out the weapon. The same one from the video. Black steel. Heavy truth. "This is the gun that killed Metal."

"Alright," I said, easing back. "That was a bluff. I made it up."

He raised the barrel. "I don't think they've seen the tape either."

"You want to bet your life on that?"

"Yeah," he replied knowing any outcome for him would end in darkness.

"Mikey!" I shouted.

"Drop it, David!" Mikey stepped from the shadows, gun leveled and voice sharp. No hesitation.

"You called the cops?" David's voice cracked as he began pacing, gun trembling in his grip. "She knows. She knows too much."

"David," Mikey said calmly. "Nobody else needs to get hurt. Put it down. We can figure this out."

David stopped. Still. Too still.

"Somebody always gets hurt," he said.

He looked at me. Then he spun.

Mikey fired.

Too slow.

David's shot hit center mass twice. Mikey collapsed.

I roared and tackled David to the pavement. The gun skidded away.

I threw punches like they were therapy. My knuckles split. Blood spattered. I wanted him to hurt.

He head-butted me. My nose exploded in red and pain. I stumbled back and he took advantage pounding my ribs, my shoulder.

I kicked him off and scrambled to my feet. He did too. His eyes locked on the gun. He dove for it.

I reached down to my ankle. Pulled my .38 from the holster and raised it.

Grabbing the fallen weapon, David turned, raising the cannon at me.

I fired six times.

Every round found home.

He stood frozen, blood blooming across his chest. He blinked. His knees buckled.

"She knows," he whispered. Then he collapsed like a dying prayer.

I dropped my arm. My hand throbbed and blood flowed freely down my arm and onto the pavement. My chest heaved.

I looked past David's body and saw Mikey lying still on the pavement, gun loose in his hand.

"MIKEY!"

I ran to him and dropped to my knees. His shirt was soaked with blood.

My stomach folded in on itself as I tore it open expecting the worst.

Kevlar. Black and bruised but intact.

Two angry swellings had already bloomed across his chest, purplish-blue and pulsing. One bruise had ruptured a vessel just above his collarbone, leaking blood that had spread across his shirt like a headline. It was enough to make me think I'd lost him.

"You just laid there and let me think you were dead?"

He groaned. "This counts as the hard part, right?"

"Hard part?" I laughed, then winced. "Look at my face."

He peeked up through one eye. "Honestly? It's an improvement."

I dropped beside him, the adrenaline crash hitting all at once. "You're a real bastard."

"Better than a dead one," he muttered, undoing the vest straps with one hand.

Sirens echoed through the alley now, rising fast.

"Your friends are coming."

CHAPTER 12

It'd been a week since the night the club turned into a war zone. I was back at the diner, same booth, same worn-down seat, same stack of pancakes pretending to be dinner. Nothing says healing like syrup and carbs.

My nose was still sore. Mikey claimed the head-butt improved my face. "Women love a man with scars," he'd said. That might explain why he had the dating life of a deflated balloon. I heard he was up for a medal for "valor in the line of fire" or some bureaucratic nonsense. He wouldn't admit it, but I knew it mattered to him. It should.

I'd called Mary the morning after it all went down. Told her the whole mess about how David went off the rails, how Mikey took two slugs to the chest and lived to complain about it. She said she'd known David, but not the full story. Claimed she didn't realize just how deep he'd sunk, or how far his obsession went.

Maybe she was telling the truth. Maybe she wasn't. Either way, Stephanie ended up dead, David ended up worse, and the world kept spinning like it didn't care.

The waitress dropped my check. I stared at it like it was mocking me.

"Is this part of the expenses?" a familiar voice asked.

I looked up. Mary stood there, a walking contradiction with a soft smile, sharp edges, and a blue dress that made my concentration crawl off the table and hide somewhere under the booth.

"The case ended last week," I said.

"Then I guess I'm not your client anymore," she replied, sliding into the seat across from me.

"That's true."

She smiled slow and dangerous. "Then I guess the 'no dating clients' rule doesn't apply."

"Lucky for you, I never had that rule."

"I was hoping you'd say that." She took a sip from my glass, like it belonged to her.

My phone buzzed. Mikey. Of course.

I let it ring once, twice.

"You're not going to answer that?" she asked, eyes teasing.

"It can wait."

"Take it," she said, nudging it toward me. "I'm not going anywhere."

I picked up the phone with a sigh. "Yeah?"

"Don't sound so thrilled," Mikey said.

"You've got impeccable timing."

"Save the charm. I need you down at the morgue. Now."

"Something new?" I asked wanting the call to be over.

"Unfortunately, no," Mikey responded.

I looked up at Mary who was watching me as if she could hear the conversation and already knew how things were changing. "We already wrapped this, Mikey. Case closed. The bad guy's dead."

"No. Case paused. This goes deeper."

His voice was off, too serious, even for him.

"What aren't you telling me?"

"There's a lot I'm not telling you. Just get here. Now." He hung up.

Mary watched me closely. The playfulness in her eyes faded. "Something wrong?"

"Mikey. Said there's something else on Stephanie's case."

"What kind of something?"

"He wouldn't say."

Her expression flickered, gone in a blink, but I caught it. Concern? Guilt? Or something darker? Before I could ask, the flirtation returned.

"Be careful," she said. "Let me know when you're done playing detective."

"Sure," I said with a crooked smile. "I'll call you when I'm free."

"You better." She stood and vanished out the front door.

I dropped cash on the table and hoped I left enough for the waitress to fake a smile. My car was around back. The morgue wasn't far, but whatever was waiting there wasn't going to smell like closure.

The autopsy room looked the same as it always did. Fluorescent, sterile, and vaguely sinister. Mikey stood next to one of the slabs. Dr. Milchin was practically bouncing.

"Steven!" he said like I was his long-lost prom date. "Always a pleasure!"

"Doctor," I said. "You seem chipper. Find a new hobby that isn't corpses?"

"Oh, Steven, there's always something exciting happening in my world!"

"I'm afraid to ask."

"Come over here," Mikey said, nodding toward the table.

The body was David. Cold. Cut and stitched back together like a bad memory.

"Bullets did the job," Mikey said, "but turns out he was already on the clock."

I rubbed my eyes. "What, cancer? Some other disease?"

"Something stranger," Milchin said, eyes twinkling like a kid unwrapping a gift. "His organs were killing themselves. Swelling and beginning to shut down. If the bullets hadn't stopped him, his own body would have eventually."

"Sounds like bad genetics," I replied still waiting for the punch-line.

"At first I thought so too. But this wasn't natural. We've had a spike of other bodies coming in with the same types of internal collapse. Organs exploding from the inside like overripe fruit."

"How many?"

"Five a week. Maybe more."

Mikey cut in. "We're talking organ failure on a mass scale."

I frowned. "Drugs?"

"Yes," Milchin said, giddy again. "Toxicology reports showed traces of poison, but nothing consistent—until I ran tests across several compounds. Some reacted differently depending on whether they were liquid or vapor."

"What are you saying?"

"He's saying it's a new drug," Mikey replied. "Something we've never seen. Hits like coke, burns like meth, hallucinates like acid, and sticks around longer than all three."

"It's called Mayhem," Milchin added with a smile that didn't match the subject. "I don't know who named it but I think they were spot on!"

"Perfect," I muttered. "Street name or side effect?"

"Both," Mikey said. "David was strung out on it. Metal too. Bolt? He had a bottle of something that fits the chemical signature. Remember all the empty water bottles you told me about?"

My mind started to click.

David's apartment. Metal's garage. The trash at the club.

"I saw it," I said. "Didn't know what it was."

"Now you do," Mikey said. "This drug isn't just frying brains. It's feeding paranoia, violence and obsession. They don't sleep. They barely feel pain. And when it's over, their bodies just quit."

"Why haven't the feds stepped in?"

"They don't see a new threat. Just a bad remix of old poisons. Until it hits national headlines, it's not their problem."

"Just ours," I said.

Mikey nodded. "We need to find the supply. Cut it off before the city turns into a war zone."

I exhaled. This thing had started with a dead girl in a canal. Now it was spreading like a sickness.

"Where do we start?"

Mikey looked at me.

"We go back to the beginning."

Milchin waved as we turned to leave. "Good luck, boys!"

"Doc," I said over my shoulder as we began to leave, "don't forget, get a hobby."

"Will do," he said. "I'll think I'll try baking. I might even have some muffins ready next time we see each other!"

CHAPTER 13

Before getting to Metal's apartment, we made a pit stop at my office. I told Mikey I needed to "grab something." Truth was, I was done playing tourist in hell with nothing but sharp words and wishful thinking.

He stayed in the car while I went in and pulled my Glock 19 from the bottom drawer. Two extra mags, just in case. The OTF knife joined it in my coat pocket. Fast deploy, easy to hide. Not that I wanted to use any of it but I'd rather be ready and disappointed than hopeful and dead.

Metal's apartment hadn't changed much. Rundown. Forgotten. This time we approached from the back. The doorman with the brick fists was gone. Maybe recovering from the last time he and I had a disagreement about manners.

We circled around back. I didn't want company. I also didn't want to knock, but Mikey insisted saying something about it being procedure.

After five minutes of knocking and pretending to be polite, I'd had enough.

"We should come back later with a warrant," Mikey said.

"We should get in now."

"Nobody's home."

"Exactly."

"That's a felony."

"Only if someone catches us."

He groaned. He didn't like it, but I wasn't in the mood for red tape.

I leaned in and listened.

"Sshh," I said, ear to the door. "You hear that?"

"No."

"Sounds like someone's in distress. Possibly yelling 'probable cause.'"

I kicked the door. It gave way like an invitation. Mikey followed me in, annoyed but armed. We cleared the apartment fast.

Mikey holstered his weapon. "There's nobody here."

"I never claimed to be clairvoyant."

The place looked like a water bottling plant had exploded. Clear bottles were everywhere. No labels. Just enough residue to hint at what had been inside. Mikey picked one up with gloved hands.

"Mayhem, I'll bet," he said. "I'll get this tested."

"Look around," I said, motioning to the chaos. "This isn't some junkie stash. This is packaging. Someone was prepping these for distribution."

Mikey crouched near a rust-colored stain soaked into the floorboards.

"That looks like blood."

"Bullet hole too," I said pointing next to him.

"You were here," he said without looking up at me.

"I'm here now."

"Would I find your fingerprints in this place?"

"Sure. I've been touching all kinds of things since we walked in. Probably licked a doorknob, too. Bad habits. You know me, no impulse control."

He stood and stared at me, hard. "This is a crime scene. After I run that for Mayhem, I'll have a warrant. We'll tear this place apart."

I gave him a smirk I didn't feel. "Let me know when you find something that tells us what we're really up against."

He made a call for backup and a warrant. We both wandered through the mess in tense silence. I poked around the kitchen, ignoring his "don't touch anything" warning the same way I ignore expiration dates on milk. I used a paper towel like a proper criminal and kept looking.

Bottles. Wrappers. Caps. But in the corner, something caught my eye. It was clear plastic with a silver dove with a branch stamped on the inside.

My heart dropped.

Mary's necklace.

Her voice echoed in my head. Better things to come. My stomach sank like a weighted corpse.

I pocketed it.

Mikey came up behind me. "Find something?"

"Just mess."

He wasn't buying it.

"They found a case of Mayhem," he said. "During a traffic stop. There was a silver dove with an olive branch in its mouth on the packaging. Someone's trying to get brand recognition."

I pulled the plastic from my pocket and handed it over. "This was in the corner."

He turned it over. Studied it.

"You were going to pocket this?"

"I did pocket it. Now, I just handed it to you."

He wasn't amused. "Steve, this is evidence."

"I know. That's why I gave it to you. Eventually."

"You're starting to worry me."

"You should be worried." I paused. "Because I think I know who's behind all this."

"Go on."

"Mary."

Mikey blinked. "Mary? As in?"

"As in Stephanie's best friend. My client. The woman we've been circling since day one."

He didn't want to hear it. He rubbed his face like the truth gave him migraines.

"That's thin, Steve."

"I don't want to believe it either," I said. "But it's her. She wore that necklace. Same dove. She's tied to everyone involved. Metal, Stephanie, and indirectly, David." She'd played me. Maybe not the whole time but long enough. And I'd let her. She had the kind of pull that reached past reason, past instinct. She wasn't just a lead anymore. She was the weight around my neck.

"She never even mentioned David before and he never mentioned her."

"He referred to someone else. It was always 'she.' Always vague. It was her."

Mikey looked away, quiet for a moment. "So what's our move?"

"We need to talk to her. Now."

"I can't bring her in on conjecture."

"You don't have to. I'll talk. You watch."

He nodded reluctantly. "Fine. But I've got crime scene investigators coming, and a judge signing off on a warrant. I'll call you when I've got something solid."

"Be quick about it."

"I'll need a ride."

"Get one from patrol. I've got things to do." I left without waiting for a goodbye.

As I hit the street, my phone rang.

"Hello, Mr. Deveroux," Mary purred. Colder this time. Less velvet, more ice.

"Mary."

"How's the investigation going?"

"Limping along."

"No need to lie. I imagine you've seen things. Perhaps you even found something of interest in that filthy apartment."

"You always this hands-on with your employees?"

"Only the ones I like." She sighed slow and sensual. "You were never supposed to be part of this. At least, not past Stephanie."

"Then why the charm campaign? Why hire me to look into everything if you didn't want me to find out about your involvement?"

"Because you were useful, Steve. And entertaining."

"You used me."

"Don't sound so wounded. We all use people. You used Mikey."

I said nothing because it was true.

"Ask your questions," she said, voice velvet again.

"Is this about just Stephanie?"

"It didn't start with her. But she made it... complicated."

"And David?"

"He fell in love. That made him dangerous."

"Were you going to have him killed?"

"He died because he couldn't see the difference between devotion and delusion. Whether or not I was going to remove him from the situation is no longer important. You killed him. I suppose I should buy you a drink." She wasn't emotional about it at all. She was calculating, like setting up pieces in a chess game and knowing which ones needed to be sacrificed.

I paused. "You going to kill me too?"

"I don't want to. I like you."

"Funny way of showing it."

"This is your warning, Steve. Let it go. Leave it be."

I could hear the crack in her voice, just a hairline fracture. Regret, maybe. Or hesitation.

"You can still walk away," she added. "Please."

"For someone so cold, you're suddenly sentimental."

Another silence.

Then: "Goodbye, Steven. Remember, this is your warning."

The line went dead.

A gunshot rang out behind me.

I turned and ran back into the apartment building and through the busted door.

Mikey was on the floor. Blood soaking the wood.

And Mary's warning still echoed in my head.

You were never supposed to be part of this.

CHAPTER 14

The hum of hospital machinery filled the void of the room like a whisper from the reaper. Steady, indifferent, inevitable. Mikey's heart monitor beeped slow and weak, but it was there. That counted for something.

After I found him bleeding on the floor, I'd called 911 and did what I could to keep the red inside. The ambulance had shown fast, but not fast enough for my nerves. His blood still crusted under my nails. This time, I hadn't charged a shooter. I'd just knelt and listened to him breathe like it was the last song I'd ever hear.

The surgery took four hours. The bullet missed everything vital somehow. Either the shooter had a difficulty focusing and bad aim, or divine intervention had a sick sense of humor.

Now he lay there, shoulder wrapped, skin pale. Breathing. Fighting. Just like always.

I was drifting off when his voice dragged me back.

"You look like shit."

I snapped upright. Mikey was awake, smiling like a man who forgot he'd been shot.

"You look worse," I said.

"Just like after those atomic burritos on the all-nighter."

"You dared me to eat two."

"I begged you not to."

"Your windows were busted."

"They weren't. You locked them."

We laughed. It was brief, broken, but it felt human. The kind of moment you miss before the world goes dark and complicated.

"So should I ask what happened?" he winced, eyeing his bandages.

"Probably not. I think Mary shot you. Or, at least, had someone shoot you."

"Seriously?"

"She told me to drop the case. I said no. She said she'd get persuasive. Then, bang. You dropped."

"You're awful at bedtime stories."

"I haven't told anyone. Every cop in town's been in here asking questions. Told them they'd hear it from you."

"Bet they loved that."

"I'm a fan favorite."

He tried to sit up but failed.

"You're out of the game for now," I said holding up my hand and easing him back onto the bed.

He sighed. "So what now?"

"Now I find her. I find the shooter. Then I break something that deserves to be broken."

He didn't answer right away.

"You can't."

"Why?"

He paused.

"Mary doesn't exist."

I blinked.

"Her name is Kathy Brennerman. She came up out of nowhere six months ago. ID, fake. Job? Fake. Social? Fake. I looked deeper. I had a facial recognition done through NCIC, the Nation Criminal Information Network, and ran her fingerprints from when Stephanie's apartment when the investigation started. Apparently she was arrested for a DUI about seven years ago in Texas. She shares an account with a woman named Sandra. Most likely her mother. Nursing home says Kathy pays the bills."

"How long have you known all this?" I asked.

Mikey looked away, then back.

"Since the night after Stephanie's body came in. Something didn't sit right. Her friend Mary was too polished. Too careful. So I started digging quietly. Changing your name doesn't mean your guilty of anything. People change their names all the time for different reasons. I didn't want to tell you until I had something concrete. I figured the less you knew, the less things had a chance of going haywire."

"Thanks for the faith."

"You're welcome. Turns out keeping it quiet didn't help much anyway."

"So she's a devoted daughter who happens to deal a body-melting drug?"

"Doesn't add up, right?"

"She's playing a deeper game."

"Exactly. And now you're a piece on her board."

I grabbed my jacket and started for the door.

"You going rogue?" Mikey asked.

"I'm not built for waiting rooms."

"Watch your step. This thing's bigger than we thought. Multiple Mayhem drops. Doogle's got a task force now. He's good, but even good cops lose their grip."

"You trust him? I never worked with Doogle," I said. "He was vice when I was narcotics. We didn't cross paths, but I knew the name."

"He's a bit of a dick. But a good one. I trust him."

I nodded. "Then I'll feed what I find to you, and you filter it to him."

He nodded back and I stepped out.

The hospital foyer hit me like a bucket of cold water. Uniforms and plainclothes wall to wall. Cops from Homicide, Narcs, Vice and Patrol. Conversations hushed as I passed. Heads turned and eyes lingered.

It was colder than any crime scene I'd ever walked into.

I used to be one of them. Now I was a question mark in a filthy suit.

Most of these guys knew my past. Some owed me drinks. Some owed me punches. And a few were still mourning friends I'd put behind bars or into the ground. Trust wasn't just scarce here. It was extinct.

I kept my chin up, eyes forward. Their stares clung to my back like guilt.

Mikey had been shot. People were dead. And every hour brought us closer to something worse.

I was going to find answers. Even if I had to drag every last one of them into the light myself.

There were still empty cells in the prison and open drawers at the morgue.

CHAPTER 15

I thought about going back to Kathy's apartment. Maybe dig through the wreckage. But the place had already been picked clean by the department. Evidence bags, shoe covers, latex gloves, and official contamination. Whatever clues had lived there were long dead or gone by now.

Mikey had mentioned something that stuck with me. Shipments of

Mayhem turning up all over town, all cut the same way. Different sellers, same poison. That meant one thing: common origin. Maybe even a single cook. If I couldn't find Kathy, I could still follow the product.

I walked. The city got darker the farther I went. Concrete cracked like old bones. Streetlights flickered and hissed above sidewalks where weeds grew like accusations. I didn't belong there but with Mikey's dried blood still on my shirt and enough bruises to look the part, I passed as a local.

I tucked myself into the doorway of an abandoned department store. Broken glass crunched beneath my heel. I watched.

Two dealers stood on the corner like they owned it. The uniforms were street casual. Hoodies, worn jeans, and thousand-yard stares. A car slowed. One of them leaned in, spoke low. The other retrieved something from a brown paper bag hidden behind a busted streetlight. The handoff was fast. Clean. Efficient.

A classic street deal. And not a single cop in sight. Not surprising as this part of the city had been left behind long ago. Cops only came out here when there were bodies. Sometimes not even then.

I waited through three more deals. Watched their rhythm. Noticed who carried and who played lookout. When I moved, I moved slow as I crossed the street a block down and limped slightly, favoring the strong leg. Just pathetic enough to be ignored. Just weird enough to be noticed.

The tall one eyed me like I was a lost dog. "Looks like you had a bad day, banker man," he said.

His buddy, who was shorter, wiry, and apparently the hyena of the two, started circling me. I didn't react. Just kept my head down and voice low.

"I'm looking for something."

"We all looking for something, banker man," he said with a grin full of bad ideas. "Problem is, you dig deep enough, you might find something that buries you."

He stepped closer, gave me a sniff like I was dinner. His breath hit me like spoiled meat and rotgut liquor. I held my breath and held my ground.

"I can pay," I said, lifting my eyes.

That got their attention. The shorter one posted up against the wall. The tall one gave me the gold-tooth grin and said, "Nothing's free, but everything's for sale. The only question is how much you're willing to bleed."

"I'll pay what it costs."

He gave me a long look. Calculating. Then smiled like I'd just bought a ticket to the circus.

"You got cash?" he asked. "Our card reader's busted."

I pulled out a roll. A fat one. Looked impressive, but it was mostly singles sandwiched between a pair of twenties. Still, his eyes widened.

"Damn," he said. "You looking to forget, or trying to meet Jesus early?"

"My girl lied to me," I said, voice brittle. "She wasn't what I thought."

"Been there," he chuckled. "You want something to make the pain float? I got you."

"Actually," I said, "I had something else in mind."

He blinked. "Is that so?"

"Yeah. I met the guy."

"There's always a guy."

"There were a few. Things didn't end well." I motioned to the dried blood. "I need something stronger."

He cocked his head. "Powder or crystal?"

I shook mine. "I heard about something different."

He paused, reading me again. "I don't know what you mean."

I let the silence stretch.

Then I said it: "Mayhem."

The word sucked the heat out of the air. They exchanged a glance. His easy swagger evaporated.

"Don't know what that is," he said too fast. "You better get to stepping."

"Bullshit," I replied straightening up. I dropped the act and my limp vanished. The stare changed. "You either have it or you know who does. I'm not here to play games."

He stepped back, bristling. "You got a mouth on you."

He pulled a switchblade, popped the blade fast and held it up like it should mean something to me. "Maybe I take your money and leave you with a real limp that matches your story."

His buddy joined him, trying to double the threat. I didn't flinch.

"Can't do that," I said. "I came for answers and I don't intend to leave empty-handed."

He rotated the blade, letting light catch the edge. I shifted my weight, ready for the lunge. He had the look of a man who'd watched a lot of prison movies but never starred in one.

"Last warning," he said.

"No," I said. "This is yours."

He stepped forward and I drew.

The Glock barked once.

His shin exploded and he dropped like a sack of bricks, screaming, cursing, and crying like the tough guy act had never existed.

His partner froze. Young and skinny. His eyes were huge. "We don't have it!" he blurted, voice cracking. "Cops came by last week. Took the stash. Swear!"

"You know who supplies it?"

"I don't know!"

I grabbed the bleeding one by the collar, hauled him up, and pistol-whipped him hard across the jaw. He went limp and I let him crumple.

"Start talking," I told the kid.

"I, I don't have any," he stammered, hands up. "But I know who does!"

"Then start walking."

He nodded, fast, and took off down the block.

I followed, gun low at my side.

Still hungry for names.

Still bleeding for truth.

CHAPTER 16

"I'm telling you, there's no other records of a Kathy Brennerman. Except for the DUI, she has no criminal record. I'm having a difficult time finding any other records prior to that as well," Mikey said through a gravel-rough phone connection. "It's like she just stopped existing."

He sounded exhausted. Hospital beds will do that to a man, especially when he's working homicide from behind an IV pole.

"I'm surprised you got that far," I replied listening to him typing on a laptop someone had brought to his hospital room. "But it just adds more questions like why lie? Why use a new name if you don't have a criminal record? What's she really doing in this city, and how's she wrapped up in Mayhem?"

I heard a sigh on the other end, tired and hollow.

"Thanks for summarizing the case we're actively working," Mikey said. "I'm digging into her mom's history. There's something there, I can feel it."

"You're chasing ghosts, Mikey. She's been running this con a while.

Whatever this is, it didn't start with Stephanie, and it won't end with her either."

"You saying she's in danger?"

"She shot you, and I'm hunting her. Yeah, she's in danger."

"That sounded like a mild threat."

"I'm feeling pretty mild about it."

"Steve, listen," he paused, "we're trying to arrest her. Not bury her."

"Speak for the badge. I'm just trying to clean up the mess."

"Don't do anything stupid."

"That ship's been burned to the waterline."

"I've looped in Doogle. I told him to meet you."

"You didn't mention he was old or came with backup," I said, pulling into the empty lot. Doogle looked like he'd been carved from stone and left in the sun to age. Mid-fifties, hard lines in his face, patrol blues that didn't forgive the years. His partner was younger, built like a linebacker, and carrying the same permanent scowl.

"He's a pain," Mikey admitted, "but he gets results."

"You know him well?"

"We've crossed paths on a few cases. He's pulled through every time."

"That's reassuring. I'll call you after."

He tried to say something else, but I killed the line.

I stepped out of the car and walked toward the two statues waiting for me. They didn't move. Didn't blink. The tension was thicker than Kevlar.

"Doogle?" I asked.

"Lieutenant Doogle," he snapped back.

So that's how it was gonna be. "I'm Steve Deveroux."

"I know who you are," he said, tone flat and clinical. "Officer Jergensen already briefed me. He told me everything you've done."

"I hope not everything. That'd be awkward." Nothing. No smile. Not even a twitch from his partner. "Okay, no foreplay then. I assume we're working together?"

"No," Doogle said. "We're investigating this case. You're not."

"I've been following leads since this thing started. Mikey must've told you,"

"It's no longer his call. It's mine."

My smile dropped. "What's your problem, Doogle? You don't even know me, but you seem real eager to shut me down. I used to wear the badge too, you know."

"I know all about you, Deveroux. You worked narcotics, homicide, and then major crimes. You got too curious about things you weren't supposed to touch and things that weren't there. Started asking questions about your own people. Got them dragged through internal. Some got fired. Some got killed. And then you? You resigned. In lieu of being fired, I'm guessing."

"I walked away."

"Right into your little PI fantasy. Well, that fantasy got Jergensen shot."

His partner, Jimmy, cracked a grin.

"What's your deal?" I asked him. "You find a mint in your pocket, or you just constipated with attitude?"

The grin dropped.

"People are talking," Jimmy said. "Word like 'perjury' and 'rat' are getting thrown around."

"Right. Are they getting tossed around as much as your mother?"

He moved. Fast.

He threw the first punch, I gave him the second. We hit the pavement hard. Doogle grabbed him before it escalated further and yanked him back like a leash on a rabid dog.

"Cut the shit!" he barked. "You're wasting my time, Deveroux. Just give me what you've got."

I dusted myself off. "That feels like assault."

"You have something to share, or are we done?"

I wanted to lie. Wanted to walk away. But Mikey asked me to play nice for now.

"There's a bar," I said.

"There's a lot of bars."

"It's called Comfort Cove. It's a dive joint. Rotten atmosphere. I'm sure there's more going on there than we know."

"Anyone specific we should be watching there?" Doogle asked.

I thought of Metal, his scorched corpse slumped in the garage.

"Maybe the bartender."

"We've checked that place," Jimmy cut in. "It's clean."

"You been there?" Doogle asked, looking over at his partner. A brief show of surprise hinted on his face causing Jimmy explain more.

"No. Conners and Jensen handled it. They were there on another matter but there wasn't anything to report."

"You need a tetanus shot just to look at that place," I said. "Clean isn't the word I'd use." It seemed a bit too convenient that the place had already been looked into and odd that nothing was found.

Doogle continued to look at Jimmy, something unspoken passed between them. A beat of hesitation. Doubt.

Then he turned back to me.

"You're done here. I don't want to see you near this case again."

"Too bad," I said. "I'm not finished."

"Take a hint, asshole," Jimmy growled. "Nobody wants your help."

"I'm shocked," I said. "That's what I told your mother the last time I saw her."

That did it.

Jimmy lunged again. We went down, fists flying. Doogle had to pry him off. Again. I quickly stood back up. My ribs were screaming and the bandages on my hand needed changing. I was never going to heal.

"Keep your dog leashed, Lieutenant, or I file on excessive force."

Doogle smiled like a man holding a loaded dice.

"From what I saw, you went for his gun. Looked justified."

Dirty.

"Really?"

"Maybe. Or maybe nothing happened. But as I recall, you were just leaving, right?"

I wiped blood from my lip. "Sure. I'll find something else to do with my time."

"Good. Smarter than you look."

They turned and walked off. I watched as they got into their cruiser and peeled out of the lot like it they actually had somewhere to go.

As soon as the disappeared into the city, I pulled Jimmy's wallet from my coat pocket and flipped it open.

Badge. ID.

"Officer James Stewart," I read aloud. "Merry Christmas to me."

CHAPTER 17

Direct confrontation was off the table. I'd taken too many hits, some from scumbags in alleys, others from men who wore badges and pretended they were better than everyone else. Either way, my body ached, and my nerves felt like frayed wire humming under skin.

I sat in my car down the street from the Comfort Cove, stewing in the stale stink of fast food wrappers and regret. The bar was shuttered for the night. A flickering streetlamp cast shadows over the cracked pavement. I'd been here for hours, watching and thinking. Piecing together the busted puzzle in my head with nothing but bent corners and missing pieces.

I'd meant to call it a night and go home. Pretend I wasn't bleeding under the skin. But just as I reached for the ignition, the door to the Cove opened and out stepped Louis the bartender. Big, bald, and uglier than last time. His face was dotted with bandages like someone had taught him a lesson using a bottle and bad intentions.

He locked up, shuffled to a battered brown pickup, and pulled away. I didn't have a plan, but I had time and a bad habit of following trouble.

Louis made a detour through a 24-hour taco shack, loaded up a paper bag with something guaranteed to ruin a man's insides, then rolled out toward the docks.

I followed at a generous distance.

The industrial zone looked like it had been abandoned sometime in the last century.

Row after row of warehouse corpses, their rusted skins peeled back by wind and sea air. Chain-link fences sagged. Weeds climbed through concrete cracks like they had a grudge.

Louis pulled through a rusted gate into a fenced yard and parked in front of a corrugated metal building that looked like it had been condemned in another lifetime. One sickly light buzzed over the entrance, doing a poor job of pretending the place was secure.

I killed my headlights and parked a block down. From here, I could smell the ocean. Salt, oil, dead fish, and rotting ambition.

The place looked quiet. No security patrols. No cameras that I could see, though that didn't mean they weren't there.

Two other trucks sat in the lot, both coated in grime thick enough to suggest they hadn't moved in weeks. Ghosts with license plates.

I moved in, slow and low, sticking to shadows and making the night work for me. I circled the building until I found the rear loading area. A rust-scarred roll-up door sat dead center, its bottom edge chewed through by time. A new padlock clung to it like a sore thumb. Whatever was inside, they wanted it quiet.

Next to the garage door was a steel ladder bolted into the wall and streaked with salt corrosion. I grabbed it and climbed.

The roof was flat, uneven, and slick with gull crap. A single access door stood ajar at the top. No lock. Either lazy or arrogant.

I slipped inside.

The building was a hollowed-out carcass with long halls, echoing emptiness, fluorescent lights that didn't buzz so much as wheeze like dying lungs. As I crept down toward the lower level, the silence broke.

Voices. Machinery. Movement.

I cracked a door.

The room beyond was a repurposed loading dock lit bright and white in stark contrast to its surroundings. Dozens of pallets were stacked floor to ceiling with water bottles. Trucks backed into bays, their cargo doors yawning like open wounds. Men in gloves loaded crates with mechanical precision.

And then there was the other side was the chemistry set. Long tables lined with vials, burners, and tubes. White coats, surgical masks, chemical stains. The kind of setup that didn't get built unless someone planned to make a fortune or a war. Possibly both.

In the center of it all, Louis paced with the nervous authority of a man pretending to be in charge. He was barking at a group of better-dressed men with sharper suits and cleaner hands. Corporate types. They watched him without flinching, nodded when appropriate. Cold eyes. Calculating.

The crates that were being loaded weren't labeled Mayhem. Of course they weren't. They said Inter-ative Immuno Relief – Non-Sterile Vials. Looked official. FDA seals. Clinical fonts. But I'd seen the formula written in a coroner's report. This wasn't relief. It was chaos bottled in batch lots.

Mayhem didn't hit the streets through pushers. At least not in the beginning. It hit like a whisper beginning with doctors, clinics and pain management fronts. The real money didn't come from addicts. It came from the middle class trying to sleep, cope, survive.

My eyes drifted to the vans. The vans displayed their company: Inter-ative

Pharmaceuticals. A company with a public face, city contracts, and a PR department on speed dial. All of it just a front for a chemical weapon masked as a drug.

Mayhem wasn't just a street poison. It was a business.

I pulled out my phone. Snapped photos. They weren't going to win awards, but they'd get the point across.

I stayed until the last van drove off, eight in total. All filled with product. All gone in different directions.

Then I turned and climbed out the way I came.

When I got back to my car, I dialed Mikey. Straight to voicemail.

"Mikey," I said, low and urgent. "I found it. The whole damn operation. Mayhem's being cooked, bottled, and moved out of the docks. Inter-ative Pharmaceuticals is the front. Call me as soon as you can. And by the way, Doogle's still a huge dick."

Twenty minutes later I stepped into his room with bagels and two drinks.

"Room service?" he asked.

"Don't flatter yourself. It's all mine."

"Touching."

I handed him one. "Sip carefully. I didn't ask what it was."

"Could be poison."

"Wouldn't that be ironic?"

He grunted. "So what do you got?"

I sat down and launched in. "Last night I tailed Louis. He went to a warehouse at the docks. The place looked abandoned from the outside. But inside? Full-blown operation. Lab, packaging line, trucks. I watched eight vans drive off. Label: Inter-ative Pharmaceuticals."

Mikey sat straighter. "That's huge."

"No kidding. But we've got a problem," I said.

"What?"

"It's not enough. No samples. No warrant. No one's going to accept my photos as genuine so they won't be admissible in court or probable cause for a warrant. It's going to be looked at as circumstantial, all of it."

"True. They'll ask how you got them."

"I'll tell them I broke in."

"That'll go great in court. You'll probably be charged with breaking and entering instead."

"Which is why I'm telling you," I replied. "Vouch for the photos and evidence. Say you got it from a confidential informant. A CI's information is protected so they can't make you disclose it."

He looked frustrated. "It's thin and I'm in the hospital. This is all going to Doogle and I'm not sure he's going to do anything with this if he can't verify its origins."

"And that's the problem. I don't trust him. Or his pit bull."

"Jimmy?"

"He's itching to break something, and I'm the nearest target. Doogle talks clean, at least part of the time, but he stinks of cover-up or involvement. I have figured out which."

Mikey nodded slowly. "I'm beginning to think you may be right. I've started hear things about them. Quiet stuff. Cases they closed that shouldn't be closed. Witnesses who stopped cooperating."

"They're dirty. Maybe not rotten, but cracked enough to let Mayhem slide right in."

Before he could answer, the door opened. Doogle walked in, followed by Jimmy, both dressed like they owned the place. Doogle's jaw was tight. Jimmy's knuckles were already whitening.

"What the hell are you doing here?" Doogle barked.

"Bringing breakfast to a friend," I said turning to them both. "Want a muffin?"

Jimmy stepped closer. "You don't know when to quit, do you?"

"Nope. But you do. Usually right after I hit back."

Jimmy lunged. I stepped aside, grabbed his jacket and used his momentum to twist him into the wall. Doogle moved fast, hands on Jimmy's shoulder.

"Stand down!" he hissed.

Jimmy resisted. I didn't let go.

"Now!" Doogle snapped. Then, quieter: "There are nurses outside. You want a write-up for roughing up a civilian in a hospital?"

That did it. Jimmy stepped back, seething.

Doogle turned to me. "This is your last warning. You interfere again, I'll make sure you disappear into the system so deep they'll need sonar to find you."

"Try it," I said. "But you better make it quick because I'm one call away from dropping everything I know to the press."

Doogle looked at me for a long second, then turned on his heel. "Let's go," he growled to Jimmy.

Jimmy followed, pausing to glare at me like I owed him something.

"You do that again," I said, "and you better bring backup."

They left. The room went quiet.

Mikey broke the silence. "Well. That went well."

"Next time, you make the bagel run."

My phone buzzed. Blocked number.

I answered.

"Hello, Steven," Kathy said, her voice like velvet over ice. "It appears you didn't take my advice."

CHAPTER 18

"Kathy," I said, my voice low, choosing each word like it might be my last. "You know I've never been good at letting things go."

"That's what I like about you, Steve," she said, voice like silk wrapped around steel. "One of your more charming flaws."

"Flattery's wasted on me, Kathy. But points for trying."

"I think you should calm down. You sound tense."

Her voice didn't come from the phone anymore, it came from everywhere. From inside my skull. From the empty hallway ahead.

"You can see me?"

"I told you, Steven. I see everything."

It wasn't a boast. It was a threat wrapped in perfume.

"I warned you to walk away. I'm not the only one who did."

That landed. The walls closed in. The shadows shifted. Someone was watching. Maybe everyone was. I was drowning in a game without knowing where the board started.

"What do you want?"

"More than I can have," she sighed, and for a second, there was a trace of sorrow in her tone. "But I work hard for what I can get."

"So what is it, then?" I asked, eyes darting to every face in the waiting room, trying to read the mask behind the mundane.

"You already know I won't tell you. What's the point in mystery if you give it all away?"

"You're afraid," I said. "You're scared of what I'll dig up."

"There's nothing left to dig, Steven. Nothing that'll help you."

"I know your real name. Kathy Brennerman. From Lamont, Texas. Your mother's in a home with late-stage Alzheimer's. You send her money every month. Money from your cover job."

A pause. A soft one. Thoughtful.

"You've done your homework. A little late, but not bad. Yes, the job was for show. I admit it. That was a misstep. But you're still missing pieces."

"So fill them in."

"I don't think you have as much time as you think."

The way she said it dropped a chill down my spine. I stepped into a dark alcove. I didn't like the way the walls suddenly felt closer.

"But," she continued, "since we're being honest, I'll give you something. A parting gift, if you like."

"Don't overdo the sentiment. It doesn't suit you."

"It's true about my mother. She doesn't remember me. Hasn't for years. But I was raised outside Lamont. It was a small place. Quiet and safe but not many jobs were available and everyone was struggling to get by. Then Inter-ative Pharmaceuticals showed up."

Connection.

"They built a plant and promised jobs. They saved a dying town. For a while."

"What happened?"

"They poisoned everything. The soil, the water, the people. When anyone pushed back, they got sued into the dirt. Or worse. My father died believing he was the failure. My mother stopped speaking out about them. I didn't."

Her voice was steady, but her words came with weight.

"I studied their methods. Their legal structure. The way they shielded their profits with patents and shell companies. I learned their language so I could weaponize it against them."

She paused.

"That's when I became Mary. I buried Kathy Brennerman. I infiltrated their world. First with drugs, then through relationships. Not love, leverage."

"And Stephanie?" I asked, the air thick between us.

A long silence.

"She was my roommate. My friend. She got involved with Metal who turned out to be a violent addict. She didn't tell me how bad it was until it was too late. I didn't know he was dealing Mayhem. Not until I traced one of the early batches back to him."

Her voice cracked for the first time.

"Mayhem was mine. I created it. But it was never meant for her."

I waited.

"She caught him using several times and finally decided to confront him. She wanted him to stop using or she'd leave him. She told me she was going to break up with him. I should have been with her. She died in a car."

"She died in a parking lot behind a bar," I said, quietly.

"She died because I lost control," Mary said. "Because I built a storm and thought I could stand in it without getting wet."

"You blamed Metal?"

"I blamed myself. But I knew if I walked away then, her death would be for nothing. So I kept pushing. I built the distribution network. We didn't just hand it to street dealers. That would've been sloppy. No, we sold Mayhem as a new off-label anxiety treatment to pain clinics first. Branded it as PZ-7. Made it clean. White coats and fluorescent lighting."

"Then we leaked it to the street. Slowly. Making sure it landed with the desperate and the violent. The dealers took the bait because of the money. They thought they were flipping surplus meds. By the time anyone figured out it was something else altogether, it was everywhere. I baited Inter-ative with a fix and they bought it. Hook, line, IPO."

"You let the city burn to punish one company."

"I lit a fire under a system that only responds to smoke."

I shook my head. "Innocent people have died because of what you made. That's not justice."

"No," she said. "It's survival. You're a man who's lost people, Steven. You know the weight. I've carried mine alone for too long."

"You hired me to investigate your friend's death knowing you were at the center of it."

"I needed to know how far it spread. Whether Metal acted alone. Whether Inter-ative had a part in her death also."

"And did they?"

She was quiet. Then: "Does it matter?"

Her eyes, if I could see them, would've told me the truth.

"It all comes back to me," she said. "And I'll carry that. I always have."

I stared at the phone. At the silence that followed.

"I didn't ask to be the villain," she said. "But I stopped pretending the heroes were coming." She stopped walking and waited for a brief moment. "I'll miss you."

My stomach dropped.

"You going somewhere?"

"No. But Mikey is."

My blood turned to ice.

"Please, tell him goodbye. It wasn't personal."

I dropped the phone and ran. I shoved past nurses and patients. Voices screamed behind me, but they blurred.

"Mikey!"

I rounded the corner, his room just ahead.

He looked up, eyes tired but warm.

Then the world tore apart.

A sound like the sky cracking open swallowed the hallway. Fire ripped through the corridor as glass shattered inward in a storm of light and heat. Walls folded and the floor buckled as everything became noise and flame. The force hit me like a sledgehammer. I flew backward, hit something hard, then the black took me.

I came to for a second.

Screams. Sirens. Smoke rolling like fog soaked in gasoline. A nurse stumbling, her face bleeding. Someone began dragging me. Gloved hands, shouting orders. My body jerked on a stretcher.

Out again.

Back. There were faces over me, speaking urgently but I couldn't understand what was being said. Fluorescent lights were cutting the haze. A mask was secured over my mouth. My chest was burning like someone shoved a fire inside.

Darkness.

Consciousness returned like a broken film reel. Flickering, jarring and incomplete.

Then, darkness swallowed me again.

I woke in pain.

My body was wrapped in bandages and regret. Tubes ran from me like I was a machine barely patched together. The lights hurt and my chest burned. My vision was slow to return.

A doctor in white stood at the foot of the bed. Beside her, a hard face I recognized immediately.

Lieutenant Doogle.

He didn't look like he was there to offer condolences.

"Mr. Deveroux," the doctor said, "You've been in an accident."

"No accident," I croaked. "That was a bomb. Don't insult me."

Doogle stepped forward. "You're right. It wasn't."

"Mikey?"

His eyes didn't flinch. "Officer Jergensen is dead. The bomb was placed in his room. It detonated minutes after you left."

Each word was a blade.

"I hope," I rasped, "you have a suspect in mind."

"We do," he said. "You."

I blinked. "Come again?"

"You're being detained as a person of interest in the murder of Officer Jergensen and the bombing of this hospital, which resulted in eight deaths and multiple injuries."

"That's bullshit," I snarled.

"You were with him before the shooting. You brought him to the apartment where he was first attacked. Then to the club. Now here." His voice was flat, surgical.

"You think I killed my best friend?"

"I think your recklessness got him killed."

That one cut the deepest. Because part of me believed it too.

I sank back against the bed. The room blurred. The guilt hit harder than the blast.

Mikey had trusted me. And I'd led him to his grave.

I didn't respond.

Doogle turned on his heel and left.

Later, a familiar voice broke the silence.

"Steven!" Milchin beamed, bounding into the room like a kid with a balloon.

"You here to measure me for a drawer?" I asked, voice raw.

"Not today. You're not dead yet. Although you tried really hard."

He checked my chart with cheery precision, but his eyes betrayed him. They were wet, unfocused.

"I wanted to see how you were doing."

"Lungs are holding up. The pain's constant but I'm still breathing."

"A miracle," he said brightly. "Though you owe that miracle to a wall. The blast threw you into it. Apparently it collapsed your lung. You almost didn't make it."

"I should've been in that room."

"Fate's a funny thing," he said slowly nodding in agreement.

His voice cracked on the word "fate."

"He was my friend too, Steven. Both of you... I never said it, but you matter. He mattered."

"He didn't deserve that."

Milchin nodded, then quietly cleared his throat. "They asked what you and Officer Jergensen were investigating. I told them what was already in the reports. Mayhem. Murders. Overdose spikes."

"Did you leave anything out?"

"Only what they wouldn't understand."

He leaned closer, suddenly serious.

"There's something off. When you started this I had Mayhem victims coming in daily. Then it dropped. Like completely to nothing. Like someone turned off the faucet."

"Supply dried up?"

"Or there's a cure."

That hit me sideways. "A cure?"

"Yes. And guess who has it? Inter-ative Pharmaceuticals. Of course."

My gut twisted.

"They're making billions," Milchin said. "And tomorrow they go public. Everyone who got in early? They're going to be filthy rich."

"Including Kathy's mother."

Milchin blinked. "Who?"

"Never mind," I said. "It doesn't matter. Not yet."

"Steve," he said quietly, "I don't know who this woman is, but if she took Mikey from us... she doesn't deserve peace."

"She's not getting it."

Milchin nodded his head as if knowing I was about to do something stupid, and he was all in. "What do you need?"

"I need you to reach out to any friends you may have at Inter-ative. Quietly. I need answers."

He nodded. "Discretion is my specialty."

"God help us," I muttered.

And somewhere, out in the shadows, I knew Kathy was already two moves ahead.

CHAPTER 19

Kathy must have known what might happen. It was happening too perfectly. Looking back, this wasn't a bad consolation prize. Instead of destroying a pharmaceutical giant, she'd just made her mother rich, even if her mother couldn't remember the fortune or spend it. And then, the company would collapse in bankruptcy and scandal.

The company had gone public two days ago. Stock prices tripled overnight. A few higher-ups allegedly became millionaires off their portfolios. It smelled too clean, too fast.

Milchin had called in a favor from someone inside Inter-ative Pharmaceuticals.

"Here's what I found," he said after hanging up. "No money was sent out of the city. At least not from this plant. Inter-ative was global but under several different names."

"Well, that sucks. I was putting all my eggs in that basket."

His phone buzzed again. Quick chat. Hung up.

"A few more bodies in the morgue. Might be Mayhem again," he said, too cheerful.

"Dopers clearing their stashes?"

He shrugged. "Maybe. Wanna come?"

"As fun as that sounds, I'm still being detained."

"Get your shoes ready. There's not much else they can do for you here." He waved and left.

I flipped through the hospital TV. Static. Game shows. Nonsense. Then I saw it. Doogle escorting a man in cuffs out of a corporate tower. The chyron read: Inter-ative CEO Arrested.

"Donald Jessop, CEO and owner of Inter-ative Pharmaceuticals, has been arrested for his part in a nationwide drug scheme... mastermind behind the creation and distribution of a drug with the street name of Mayhem. He was also responsible for engineering the cure in hopes of profiting off the crisis."

They were already spinning it for the cameras. Jessop the villain. The company tanked. Stocks plummeted from $180 to $2 per share.

I stopped listening. I knew the play.

My window was closing and it was time to move.

I stood and pain knifed through my ribs. My side was on fire as my lungs wheezed with each breath. The blast had left more than memories.

I crept to the interior window and looked out. The hallway was clear. Whoever had been posted to watch me was gone. Maybe chasing coffee, maybe using the can. Either way, I didn't have long.

I closed the curtain, changed into my clothes, and slid into the hall. I hugged the wall as I moved. Every opening and shadow was a threat.

I heard a voice yelling from behind me. I turned and watched as an officer was asking where the patient had gone. He pulled his radio and began to alert someone on the other side of my disappearance.

I dove into the stairwell and slammed the door behind me. My heart was pounding and I used the stair well to keep me from falling.

I needed chaos. Fast.

I yanked the fire alarm. The emergency sirens screamed as the red lights began to strobe. Nurses, patients, and staff all spilled out like ants from a burning hill. Everyone was acutely aware of the explosion and did their best to escape the possibility again.

I slipped into the tide. Just one more face in the flood.

Hours later, I sat in a car two blocks from the Comfort Cove. Always back to this dump. Like the universe was on repeat.

The place looked untouched. Jimmy had claimed they'd already looked into this place. Bull. There was no damage and no signs of a struggle. Same cracked facade. Same broken soul.

I checked my watch. I was running out of time.

I reached into the duffel on the passenger seat. Bullpup shotgun. Glock 19 on my hip. Ruger 556 in the back. I'd stashed it all at Gary's office weeks ago, back when things first got weird. He didn't know and that was the point.

If I'd left them in my place, the cops would've scooped them up with the furniture.

My head throbbed and I popped a few pills of unmarked pain killer from a bottle that was missing its label. My ribs ached. But I still had breath in my lungs, and that was enough.

Things were painful enough and I was tired of feeling.

I thought about Doogle's threats. About the guy who attacked me outside the precinct. I connected the dots. Stewart. Doogle's attack dog.

The same Jimmy Stewart.

I gritted my teeth.

I was done asking politely.

Louis was inside. And I had questions.

I floored the car.

It roared down the block, jumped the curb, and tore through the front window of the bar. Glass exploded inward. Chairs snapped and wood screamed.

Smoke, dust and chaos.

I stepped out of the car and spotted Louis standing behind the bar, wide-eyed. All the bar's patrons stared at me. Some still holding their glasses halfway in the air as they hadn't been able to take a drink due to my driving tactics. Lucky for them, they'd all been sitting at the far end of the bar and had missed becoming a bug on my windshield.

"Hi," I said, waving. "Got a couple questions for you."

He pulled a gun and opened fire.

Rounds punched into the car. Some of the customers ducked while others pulled heat. I rolled left, shotgun in hand.

When his gun ran dry, I stood and put a round of birdshot in his chest. He flew back. Not dead but hurting.

More guns. More noise. The customers had no desire to be left out of the commotion. I ducked and fired back. The bullpup barked, and men dropped.

Pain bloomed in my arm as a round ripped through my sleeve and bit me.

I ditched the shotgun after firing the last round and crawled for the Ruger in the backseat. The glass from the rear window rained down on my back as I fired through the passenger door. Through tables. Through meat.

I crawled back out the way I entered and picked off the last men from under the car.

Eight total. Seven down.

I stepped over bodies and walked to the bar.

Louis was slumped over the counter, blood blooming.

"Might've been closer than I thought with that shot," I said.

I tied a filthy rag around my arm. It stung like hell. "This better be clean," I said looking down at Louis. "I'd hate to get an infection."

"What do you want?" he asked.

"Where's Mayhem? Where's Kathy? How'd she bring down Interative?"

"I don't know."

I dropped down and punched him in the chest. He coughed blood.

"I don't have time. You talk or you die."

His face paled. "I need help."

"And a dry cleaner but I don't think you can afford either," I said. "Start talking. What did you tell Doogle?"

"Doogle? I don't know any Doogle."

I reared back for another punch.

"Wait!" he gasped. "There's no Doogle! The cop's name is Stewart!"

"Stewart?"

"Yeah. Big guy. Bad attitude. Like you."

"Flattery."

"He's been moving Mayhem for months. Streets, warehouses, then Inter-ative."

"How?" I asked, ready to punch his ticket and be done with it.

"They used a shell supply company out of Jersey to front the shipping. Legit trucks, forged manifests, chemical warehouses with front-door security and back-door firepower. The Mayhem gets cooked at the docks, branded as commercial painkillers, and then moved across state lines with FDA tags and dummy barcodes."

"And nobody asked questions?"

"They kept it small. Distributed it like boutique liquor. Just enough to seed the market, not enough to set off alarms. Inter-ative bought the silence with stock options."

"And the cure?"

"They always had it. It was a cancer drug with too many side effects so they shelved it. Then someone had the bright idea to flip the script."

"Create a disease. Sell the cure."

He nodded.

"Why did Jessop agree?"

"Billions. Wouldn't you?"

"I can barely cover my rent. How'd you get roped in?"

"Stewart's my parole officer. All of us. It's easy to force loyalty."

I stood, blood running down my arm. I hurt. My hand hurt, my chest hurt and I was tired. So much for the painkillers.

"Tell everything to Doogle when they come. Only him."

He nodded.

"One last thing. Where can I find Stewart?"

Louis lifted his head, gave a crooked smile.

The game wasn't over yet.

CHAPTER 20

Louis had informed me there was one more batch of Mayhem that Jimmy wanted moved by the parolees. It was going to be loaded onto a boat at the marina in two hours. I sat behind a large metal storage container and watched as boxes were being loaded onto a small boat. My car, with the engine smoking and shot, had almost made it the whole way to the marina. I ended up parking under an overpass and, with the guns in my bag, walked the rest of the way in. My ribs throbbed. My arm ached. I pushed through it, one foot at a time.

I was still wondering how I'd made it the whole way without being spotted when I felt the cold steel of a muzzle press into the back of my head.

"I have so many questions," Doogle said in a low gravelly voice.

I slowly turned back to look at the carbine he had aimed at me. "I'm glad you're not just jumping to conclusions. I was afraid you might think I was in the wrong and shoot me by accident."

"I do think you're in the wrong. And just because I haven't shot you yet doesn't mean I won't."

"Fair enough," I replied. "Looks like you got my message. How's our large friend?"

He lowered the gun.

"Still alive for now. Doesn't mean what he said was true."

"It adds up. I had him tell you because Mikey trusted you. Even though you're a bit of a dick, I think you're trying to do the right thing. How's your partner?"

He didn't answer right away. "After I left you at the hospital, I tried to contact him. He wouldn't answer his phone and he wasn't at the office. I went to his home and discovered left over materials that had been used in making a bomb."

"He planted the bomb on Mikey?" My blood was beginning to boil.

"That's the theory," Doogle said reluctantly. "Apparently, he grew up outside of Lamont, just like Mary. We didn't know because we didn't have any reason to look into him. They've probably known each other the whole time."

I had no words. I just sat there, letting the information sink in.

Then came the yelling from the docks.

We turned. Jimmy was barking at the parolees who were getting the last shipment in place. And next to him, Kathy. She smiled and kissed him like they were already celebrating.

"That two-timing bitch," I muttered.

Doogle raised an eyebrow.

"You know her?"

"She was a client."

"A client?"

"We had lunch."

"Lunch," he said, dragging the word out. "Is that what the kids are calling it these days?"

"I don't talk to kids and yeah, it was just lunch. Then she had Mikey shot."

That stopped him.

"You didn't want to start with that?"

"Didn't seem relevant until now. Also, I think Jimmy pulled the trigger."

He stared at the scene. "What's your plan?"

"I was thinking we shoot the bad guys," I replied.

"What?" He looked at me like I'd just kicked a puppy.

"Well just in the leg maybe. For starters. See how that works out." He just stared, mouth agape.

"Wait here," he said, walking toward his vehicle.

"Where are you going?"

"That's a stupid plan," he replied turning back towards me. "We can't just start shooting. I'm going to arrest him and he'll face whatever charges he's guilty of."

I was shocked. Since when did he worry about just arresting someone responsible for killing another cop?

"You want to waltz into the lion's den and have a heart-to-heart with the guy who nearly killed you and who definitely killed Mikey?"

"We're partners."

"You were partners," I snapped. "He replaced you and now he's running a drug empire. What part of that screams 'let's talk it out' to you? What about calling for backup?"

"It'll be too late by the time they arrive. Besides, he's got a radio and will know they're coming."

"He's dangerous," I warned. "He won't hesitate to shoot you."

"Stay here," he said, already walking away.

"You're a moron."

"So are you," he called back. "We'll get along great."

Doogle drove down to the dock. Several parolees raised their weapons. He got out slowly, hands high, calling for Jimmy. I flanked around the building, finding an unlocked side door.

Inside, the warehouse was all angles and echoes. Pallets, crates, dust, and guns. I crouched behind a stack, drew the AR-556, and waited.

Jimmy saw Doogle'and waved off a few guards. "Look who dragged himself away a desk."

Doogle slowly approached Jimmy, keeping his hands up. "I just want to know why."

"You always needed everything spelled out." Jimmy chuckled. "You were a good partner, Doogle. You really were. Loyal. Honest. Problem is, honest doesn't pay."

"So that's it?" Doogle asked. "You sold your badge for a payday?"

"Not just the badge," Jimmy said. "I sold it for her."

Kathy stepped out from the shadows.

"We planned this for years," Jimmy continued. "Since we were kids. She saw the world for what it was. I just followed her lead."

"You killed Mikey."

Jimmy's expression hardened. "That wasn't personal. I liked him, he was a good man. He was just in the way."

"Jimmy, you're throwing it all away!" Doogle shouted.

"I made millions. I'm done."

"I can't let you walk."

"I know," Jimmy said.

I was already moving. Sliding through shadows. As Jimmy turned to check the perimeter, I saw the glint of his gun.

He raised it.

I shouted. "Doogle, down!"

He ducked, but not fast enough. Jimmy fired and clipped him in the shoulder.

Doogle dropped hard.

I opened fire. Rounds erupted like a war film on fast-forward. My shots tore through three parolees before they even knew what hit them. Bullets cracked concrete and snapped past my ears. I dove and crawled through broken crates, returning fire when I could. Jimmy was still on the dock shouting orders at other parolees.

I rushed in and collided into Jimmy like a freight train. His service weapon scattered across the ground until it collided with the wooden crates. Fists flew. My ribs screamed. His elbow cracked against my jaw. I slammed my knee into his thigh. He grabbed my head and drove it into a crate.

We grappled on the dock, fists wet with blood and sweat. Doogle tried to stand, groaning.

Jimmy slammed me to the ground and kicked me in the ribs. I rolled off the edge but caught the dock with one hand.

My arm burned. My shoulder tore.

Jimmy turned back towards Doogle. He picked up his service weapon and raised it towards Doogle who was pushing himself up on one knee, trying to aim.

I pulled myself up over the ledge and swung my other arm up, knife in hand. The serrated blade of my OTF knife stabbed into Jimmy's hip and sunk in until the handle stopped it. I held onto the knife and let my weight drop, savagely ripping the blade down his leg in the process.

He howled as his leg opened up. He began to fall and turn at the same time raising the gun at my face.

BANG.

Doogle fired.

Jimmy dropped.

Blood pooled and silence followed.

I pulled myself up over the edge of the dock and breathing raggedly as I let my body collapse on the ground.

Doogle sank to the ground, holding his wound. He looked at Jimmy's body, eyes heavy. I understood. It was a confusing feeling of betrayal having your partner turn out to be a killer. "Thanks for the save," I said.

"I owed you one."

"That make us even?"

"Not even close," he muttered.

We shared a breath. Not quite a smile. But something close.

"You alright?" I asked.

"No. But I'll live."

"You're a better shot than I gave you credit for. Especially for an old guy."

"Don't make me regret it."

Kathy was gone.

I turned to Doogle. "You think she made it very far?"

"I'll be right behind you," Doogle said, nodding towards the direction she'd ran off in.

"Dammit," I said standing back to my feet. "I hate running."

"Go," Doogle said. "I got your back."

I nodded and ran.

My legs barely worked. My side was lava. But I chased the ghost that started all of this. The one I couldn't let disappear. I rounded the corner and she was waiting. The shot hit my chest, low and left. I dropped.

She stood over me, gun aimed, eyes lit not with hate but with inevitability. Her body trembled ever so slightly. Not from fear. From choice.

"You should've stayed out of this," she said.

Blood pooled under me. My vision swam, but I held her in focus. "You used me."

Mary's eyes flicked away for a moment, then returned to mine. "No. I chose you because I thought you'd understand."

"Understand what?" I coughed, the pain searing through my chest. "That this was about revenge?"

"No. About justice," she said, jaw tightening. "But the kind that works in the dark. The kind you buy in blood."

She took a breath.

"I created Mayhem. I built the pipeline. But I never wanted Stephanie dead. She wasn't part of the plan. She was the last good thing I had left. And I let her fall into Metal's arms and into that life. I didn't know he was using the drug. Not mine. Not my batches."

"You built a monster you couldn't control."

"No," she snapped. "I built a weapon. Because the system was the monster. And people like Metal? They were symptoms."

She circled slowly.

"Stephanie was more than a friend. She was my family. I never had a sister, but she filled that space."

Her voice trembled. "And when she died, I burned."

I pushed up on one elbow, pain screaming. "You don't get to rewrite this. Dozens of people are dead. Whole blocks burned. You flooded the streets with a nightmare."

"And Inter-ative is still standing," she spat. "Untouchable. They buried my town, silenced survivors, profited off the same drug that killed thousands. You think this is about ego? This is about sending a message loud enough to crack teeth in boardrooms."

"Stephanie's dead."

Her face twisted. "Don't you think I know that?"

The gun lowered an inch. Her hand shook now.

"I never meant for the innocents to die. Not the kids, not the addicts who never stood a chance. But I can't take any of it back. I can't put the fire out. It's already burned too far."

She took a step closer. "I crossed a line. I know that. And there's no going back. Not for me."

"I don't think you're evil," I said. "But you killed any chance of redemption."

She stared down at me. Not as an enemy. Not even as a man she once tried to seduce. But like a mirror showing her what she'd lost.

"I'm sorry," she whispered.

Then she raised the gun.

The shot cracked through the silence.

Mary staggered. Blood bloomed on her side.

Doogle limped forward, weapon raised, face carved from stone.

She turned back to me, eyes wide, not with pain, but disappointment.

Then she dropped.

Doogle continued to limp forward.

"You shot my girlfriend," I said looking from Kathy's fallen body over to Doogle.

"Ex-girlfriend," he replied, sliding down and sitting against a crate just opposite of me.

"Fair."

"You're not dying."

"Feels like it."

Sirens howled.

"You owe me a car," he muttered.

I laughed.

Then passed out cold.

CHAPTER 21

I sat in the diner eating French toast. After two weeks of hospital food, it tasted like redemption. Greasy, golden, soaked in syrup, and smothered in powdered sugar. I would've paid double for it and still felt like I owed the cook a handshake.

The fallout had been biblical. Kathy was dead, but she'd still won in some ways. Not all the money was recovered. What was found went straight to her mother's care facility, legally protected and untouchable. The rest had been funneled off-shore and deep into shadow accounts that even the feds couldn't trace without divine intervention.

I'd been exonerated. The grand jury didn't buy the city's narrative that I was the cause of so much destruction. Too many bodies. Too much rot. Someone had to be the one pulling the string and it wasn't me. Somehow, all my hospital bills were paid off. No one said who. I didn't ask.

Doogle was set to testify next week. He told me the prosecutors wanted to hear from me, too. But I wasn't eager to revisit every punch, bullet, and betrayal. The whole mess already sounded like something ripped out of a cheap crime novel.

He'd changed, too. Doogle was quieter now. Not softer, but heavier. He carried the weight of Jimmy's betrayal in his spine, like it twisted everything about how he saw the world. Justice used to be black and white for him. Now it was shades of ash. He didn't say it, but I knew he backed me in the end because something inside him broke and had been rebuilt with different parts. He believed me now. Or maybe he just believed in what we'd fought for.

My lungs ached if I breathed too deep. The doc told me I was one of the lucky few who'd survived a collapsed lung twice. Said I must have a horseshoe shoved somewhere dark. I didn't feel lucky. I felt tired. Hollow.

I reached into my pocket to pay for the meal and came up short. No surprise. Luck doesn't pay tabs. But Officer Jimmy Stewart had left behind a credit card. Figured the least he could do was buy me breakfast. I slipped it onto the bill.

The waitress took it without a blink. I leaned back and looked out the window. The city was gray, wet with last night's rain, and still stinking of rot. But somewhere out there, steam rose from manhole covers, street vendors opened early, and someone kissed someone else goodbye.

I'd chased a ghost through a city on fire. Lost friends. Killed men. Buried what little hope I had left in a warehouse shootout and a confession laced with tears and bullets. Kathy wasn't just a client. She was a reflection, a cracked mirror of what I could've become if I'd taken one wrong turn. There was fire behind her eyes and a pain that never cooled. In the end, she made her choice.

She wanted me to understand her before the end. In that final confrontation, her voice didn't shake. She laid it out. Her philosophy, her war. She believed the world was poison, and her fire was the cure. She wasn't just trying to get even. She was trying to balance the scales, make someone pay. Anyone.

"The world took everything from me," she said, moments before pulling the trigger. "You think laws and trials change that? You think any of them care? They're parasites in suits. I gave them justice they'd never see coming."

It wasn't just revenge. It was gospel. In her mind, she was the reckoning.

And for a second, even bleeding and on the ground, I saw her not as a killer, but as the ghost of every broken promise the city had ever made.

I knew there'd be more cases. More corpses. More desperate souls chasing poison or profit. The city was dying, sure. But not all at once. Not everywhere. Some people still clung to hope.

Me? I didn't know what I believed anymore. But I knew I wasn't done. This case had carved something out of me and left the whole wide open. The kind of scar you carry around knowing you'd never be able to make it heal.

I just wanted one more cup of coffee before the next fire started.

Outside, the wind howled.

Inside, the toast was still warm.

And I was still breathing.

ABOUT THE AUTHOR

Andrew Rowberry is an American author who lives in Utah with his wife and children. He has written several works of fiction in addition to writing and creating several sitcoms and screenplays. Andrew has spent over 20 years in the United States Navy as well as having served in several different law enforcement, investigative and consulting positions.

www.ingramcontent.com/pod-product-compliance
Lightning Source LLC
Chambersburg PA
CBHW072029170626
46811CB00008B/3002